THE
TATTOOIST
OF
AUSCHWITZ

THE
TATTOOIST
OF
AUSCHWITZ

A NOVEL

HEATHER MORRIS

HARPER

NEW YORK · LONDON · TORONTO · SYDNEY

HARPER

Originally published as *The Tattooist of Auschwitz* in Australia in 2018 by Bonnier Publishing Australia and in the UK by Bonnier Zaffre.

P.S.™ is a trademark of HarperCollins Publishers.

FIRST U.S. EDITION

Designed by Jamie Lynn Kerner
Title page photograph by taranchic / Shutterstock
Europe map by Nicolette Caven
Birkenau map © Peter Palm, Berlin/Germany

Library of Congress Cataloging-in-Publication Data has been applied for.

ISBN 978-0-06-279715-5 (pbk.)
ISBN 978-0-06-287700-0 (international edition)

19 20 PC/LSCH 20 19 18 17 16 15 14 13 12

To the memory of Lale Sokolov.
Thank you for trusting me to tell your and Gita's story.

THE
TATTOOIST
OF
AUSCHWITZ

PROLOGUE

LALE TRIES NOT TO LOOK UP. HE REACHES OUT TO TAKE THE piece of paper being handed to him. He must transfer the five digits onto the girl who held it. There is already a number there, but it has faded. He pushes the needle into her left arm, making a three, trying to be gentle. Blood oozes. But the needle hasn't gone deep enough, and he has to trace the number again. She doesn't flinch at the pain Lale knows he's inflicting. *They've been warned— say nothing, do nothing.* He wipes away the blood and rubs green ink into the wound.

"Hurry up!" Pepan whispers.

Lale is taking too long. Tattooing the arms of men is one thing; defiling the bodies of young girls is horrifying. Glancing up, Lale sees a man in a white coat slowly walking up the row of girls. Every now and then he stops to inspect the face and body of a terrified young woman. Eventually he reaches Lale. While Lale holds the arm of the girl in front of him as gently as he can, the man takes her face in his hand and turns it roughly this way and that. Lale looks up into the frightened eyes. Her lips move in readiness to speak. Lale squeezes her arm tightly to stop her. She looks at him and he mouths, "*Shh.*" The man in the white coat releases her face and walks away.

"Well done," he whispers as he sets about tattooing the remaining four digits—4 9 0 2. When he has finished, he holds on to her arm for a moment longer than necessary, looking again into her eyes. He forces a small smile. She returns a smaller one. Her eyes, however, dance before him. As he looks into them, his heart seems simultaneously to stop and to begin beating for the first time, pounding, almost threatening to burst out of his chest. He looks down at the ground and it sways beneath him. Another piece of paper is thrust at him.

"Hurry up, Lale!" Pepan whispers urgently.

When he looks up again, she is gone.

1

APRIL 1942

LALE RATTLES ACROSS THE COUNTRYSIDE, KEEPING HIS HEAD up and himself to himself. The twenty-five-year-old sees no point in getting to know the man beside him, who occasionally nods off against his shoulder; Lale doesn't push him away. He is just one among countless young men stuffed into wagons designed to transport livestock. Having been given no idea where they were headed, Lale dressed in his usual attire: a pressed suit, clean white shirt, and tie. *Always dress to impress.*

He tries to assess the dimensions of his confinement. The wagon is less than ten feet wide. But he can't see the end to gauge its length. He attempts to count the number of men on this journey with him. But with so many heads bobbing up and down, he eventually gives up. He doesn't know how many wagons there are. His back and legs ache. His face itches. The stubble reminds him that he hasn't bathed or shaved since he boarded two days ago. He is feeling less and less himself.

When the men try to engage him in conversation, he responds with words of encouragement, trying to turn their fear into hope. *We stand in shit but let us not drown in it.* Abusive remarks are muttered at him for his appearance and manner. Accusations of hailing from the upper class. "Now look where it's gotten you." He tries to shrug the words off and meet the glares with smiles. *Who am I trying to kid? I'm as scared as everyone else.*

A young man locks eyes with Lale and pushes through the scrum of bodies toward him. Some men shove him on his way through. *It's only your own space if you make it yours.*

"How can you be so calm?" the young man says. "They had rifles. The bastards pointed rifles at us and forced us into this . . . this cattle train."

Lale smiles at him. "Not what I was expecting, either."

"Where do you think we're going?"

"It doesn't matter. Just remember, we are here to keep our families safe at home."

"But what if—?"

"Don't 'what-if.' I don't know, you don't know, none of us knows. Let's just do as we're told."

"Should we try to take them when we stop, since we outnumber them?" The young man's pale face is pinched with confused aggression. His balled-up hands box pathetically in front of him.

"We have fists, they have rifles—who do you think would win that fight?"

The young man returns to silence. His shoulder is wedged into Lale's chest, and Lale can smell oil and sweat in his hair. His hands drop and hang limply by his side. "I'm Aron," he says.

"Lale."

Others around them tune in to their conversation, raising their heads toward the two men before lapsing back into silent reveries, sinking deep into their own thoughts. What they all share is fear. And youth. And their religion. Lale tries to keep his mind off theorizing about what might lie ahead. He has been told he is being taken to work for the Germans, and that is what he is planning to do. He thinks of his family back home. *Safe.* He has made the sacrifice, has no regrets. He would make it again and again to keep his beloved family at home, together.

Every hour or so, it seems, people ask him similar questions. Wearying, Lale begins to answer, "Wait and see." He is perplexed as to why the questions are directed to him. He has no special knowledge. Yes, he wears a suit and tie, but that's the only visible difference between him and the next man. *We're all in the same filthy boat.*

In the crowded wagon they can't sit, let alone lie down. Two buckets substitute for toilets. As they fill, a fight breaks out as men try to get away from the stench. The buckets are knocked over, spilling their contents. Lale clings to his suitcase, hoping that with the money and clothes he has, he might be able to buy himself out from wherever they are headed, or at the very least buy himself into a safe job. *Maybe there'll be work where I can use my languages.*

He feels lucky to have found his way to the side of the wagon. Small gaps in the slats provide him with glimpses of the passing countryside. Snatched breaths of fresh air keep the rising tide of nausea at bay. It might be springtime, but the days are filled with rain and heavy clouds. Occasionally they pass fields ablaze with spring flowers and Lale smiles to himself. Flowers. He learned from a young age, from his mother, that women love them. When would be the next time he could give a girl flowers? He takes them in, their brilliant colors flashing before his eyes, whole fields of poppies dancing in the breeze, a scarlet mass. He vows that the next flowers he gives to someone he will pick himself. It has never occurred to him that they grow wild in such large numbers. His mother had a few in her garden, but she never picked them and brought them inside. He starts a list in his head of things to do "when I get home . . ."

Another fight breaks out. Scuffling. Yells. Lale can't see what is going on, but he feels the squirming and pushing of bodies. Then there is silence. And from the gloom the words, "You killed him."

"Lucky bastard," someone mutters.

Poor bastard.

My life is too good to end in this stinkhole.

THERE ARE MANY STOPS ON THE JOURNEY, SOME LASTING MIN-utes, some hours, always outside a town or village. Occasionally Lale catches a glimpse of the station names as they speed through: Ostrava, a town he knows is close to the border of Czechoslovakia and Poland; Pszczyna, confirming that they are indeed now in Poland. The unknown question: where will they stop? Lale spends most of the time on the journey lost in thoughts about his life in Bratislava: his job, his apartment, his friends—his female friends in particular.

The train stops again. It is pitch-black; clouds block out the moon and stars completely. Does the dark portend their future? *Things are as they are. What I can see, feel, hear, and smell right now.* He sees only men like himself, young and on a journey into the unknown. He hears the grumbling of empty stomachs and the rasping of dry windpipes. He smells piss and shit and the odor of bodies too long unwashed. The men take advantage of not being thrown around to rest without the need to push and shove for a piece of turf. More than one head now rests on Lale.

Loud noises come from a few wagons back, gradually creeping closer. The men there have had enough and are going to attempt an escape. The sounds of men throwing themselves against the wooden sides of the wagon, and the banging of what must be one of the shit buckets, rouses everyone. Before long every wagon erupts, attacked from within.

"Help us or get out of the way," a large man screams at Lale as he throws himself against the side.

"Don't waste your energy," Lale replies. "If these walls could be breached, don't you think a cow would have done it?"

Several men stop their efforts, turning angrily toward him.

They process his comment. The train lurches forward. Maybe those in charge have decided movement will stop the unrest. The wagons settle down. Lale closes his eyes.

∽

LALE HAD RETURNED TO HIS PARENTS' HOME, IN KROMPACHY, Slovakia, following the news that Jews in small towns were being rounded up and transported to work for the Germans. He knew Jews were no longer allowed to work and that their businesses had been confiscated. For nearly four weeks he helped around the house, fixing things with his father and brother, building new beds for his young nephews who had outgrown their cribs. His sister was the only family member earning an income, as a seamstress. She had to travel to and from work in secret, before dawn and after dark. Her boss was prepared to take the risk for her best employee.

One evening she returned home with a poster her boss had

been asked to put in the shop window. It demanded that each Jew-ish family hand over a child aged eighteen or older to work for the German government. The whispers, the rumors about what had been happening in other towns, had finally come to Krompachy. It seemed that the Slovakian government was acquiescing further to Hitler, giving him whatever he wanted. The poster warned in bold type that if any family had such a child and did not surrender them, the whole family would be taken to a concentration camp. Max, Lale's older brother, immediately said he would go, but Lale would not hear of it. Max had a wife and two young children. He was needed at home.

Lale reported to the local government department in Krom-pachy, offering himself for transportation. The officials he dealt with had been his friends—they'd gone to school together and knew each other's families. Lale was told to make his way to Prague, report to the appropriate authorities, and await further instructions.

⁓

AFTER TWO DAYS THE CATTLE TRAIN STOPS AGAIN. THIS TIME there is a great commotion outside. Dogs are barking, orders are yelled in German, bolts are released, wagon doors clang open.

"Get down from the train, leave your possessions!" shout the soldiers. "Rush, rush, hurry up! Leave your things on the ground!" Being on the far side of the wagon, Lale is one of the last to leave. Approaching the door, he sees the body of the man killed in the skirmish. Briefly closing his eyes, he acknowledges the man's death with a quick prayer. Then he leaves the wagon, but brings with him the stench—covering his clothes, his skin, every fiber of his being. Landing on bent knees, he puts his hands on the gravel and stays crouching for several moments. Gasping. Exhausted. Painfully thirsty. Slowly rising, he looks around at the hundreds of startled men who are trying to comprehend the scene in front of them. Dogs snap and bite at those who are slow to move. Many stumble, the muscles in their legs refusing to work after days without use. Suit-cases, bundles of books, meager possessions are snatched from those who are unwilling to surrender them or simply don't under-stand the orders. They are then hit by a rifle or fist. Lale studies the men in uniform. Black and threatening. The twin lightning bolts on the collars of their jackets tell Lale who he is dealing with. The SS. Under different circumstances he might appreciate the tailoring, the fineness of the cloth, the sharpness of the cut.

He places his suitcase on the ground. *How will they know this one is mine?* With a shiver, he realizes that it's unlikely he will see the case or its contents again. He touches his hand to his heart, to the money hidden in his jacket pocket. He looks to the heavens, breathes in the fresh, cool air, and reminds himself that at least he is outdoors.

A gunshot rings out and Lale jumps. Before him stands an SS officer, weapon pointed skyward. "Move!" Lale glances back at the emptied train. Clothing blows away and books flap open. Sev-eral trucks arrive, and small boys clamber out. They snatch up the abandoned belongings and throw them into the trucks. A heavi-ness settles between Lale's shoulder blades. *Sorry, Mama, they have your books.*

The men trudge toward the looming, dirty pink-brick build-ings with picture windows. Trees line the entrances, flush with new spring growth. As Lale walks through open iron gates he looks up at the German words wrought from the metal:

ARBEIT MACHT FREI

He doesn't know where he is or what work he will be expected to do, but the idea that it will set him free has the feeling of a sick joke.

SS, rifles, dogs, his belongings taken—this he'd been unable to imagine.

"Where are we?"

Lale turns to see Aron at his side.

"The end of the line, I'd say."

Aron's face falls.

"Just do as you're told, you'll be fine." Lale knows he doesn't sound terribly convincing. He gives Aron a quick smile, which is returned. Silently, Lale tells himself to take his own advice: *Do as you're told. And always observe.*

Once inside the compound, the men are corralled into straight lines. At the head of Lale's row is an inmate with a beaten face, sitting at a small table. He wears a jacket and trousers with blue and white vertical stripes, with a green triangle on his chest. Behind him stands an SS officer, rifle at the ready.

Clouds roll in. Distant thunder claps. The men wait.

A senior officer, accompanied by an escort of soldiers, arrives at the front of the group. He has a square jaw, thin lips, and eyes hooded by bushy black brows. His uniform is plain in comparison to those guarding him. No lightning bolts. His demeanor shows that he's clearly the man in charge.

"Welcome to Auschwitz."

Lale hears the words, spoken by a mouth that barely moves, in disbelief. Having been forced from his home and transported like an animal, now surrounded by heavily armed SS, he is now being welcomed—welcomed!

"I am Commandant Rudolf Hoess. I am in charge here at Auschwitz. The gates you just walked through say: 'Work makes you free.' This is your first lesson, your only lesson. Work hard. Do as you are told, and you will go free. Disobey, and there will be consequences. Now you will be processed here, and then you will be taken to your new home: Auschwitz Two-Birkenau."

The commandant scans their faces. He begins to say something else but is interrupted by a large roll of thunder. He looks skyward, mutters a few words under his breath, flicks a dismissive hand at the men, and turns to walk away. The performance is over. His security presence hurries off after him. A clumsy display, but still intimidating.

The processing begins. Lale watches as the first prisoners are shoved forward to the tables. He's too far away to hear the short exchanges, can only watch as the seated men in pajamas write down details and hand each prisoner a small receipt. Finally it is Lale's turn. He has to provide his name, address, occupation, and parents' names. The weathered man at the table writes Lale's answers in a neat, looping script and passes him a piece of paper with a number on it. Throughout, the man never raises his head to meet Lale's eyes.

Lale looks at the number: 32407.

He shuffles along with the flow of men toward another set of tables, with another group of striped prisoners bearing the green triangle and more SS standing by. His desire for water threatens to overwhelm him. Thirsty and exhausted, he is surprised when the piece of paper is yanked from his hand. An SS officer pulls off Lale's jacket, rips his shirtsleeve, and pushes his left forearm flat on the table. He stares in disbelief as the numbers 32407 are stabbed into his skin, one after the other. The piece of wood with a needle embedded in it moves quickly and painfully. Then the man takes a rag dipped in green ink and rubs it roughly over Lale's wound.

The tattooing has taken only seconds, but Lale's shock makes time stand still. He grasps his arm, staring at the number. *How can someone do this to another human being?* He wonders if for the rest of his life, be it short or long, he will be defined by this moment, this irregular number: 32407.

A prod from a rifle butt breaks Lale's trance. He collects his jacket from the ground and stumbles forward, following the men in front into a large brick building with bench seating along the walls. It reminds him of the gymnasium at the school in Prague where he slept for five days before beginning his journey here.

"Strip."

"Faster, faster."

The SS bark out orders that the majority of the men cannot understand. Lale translates for those nearby, who pass the word along.

"Leave your clothes on the bench. They will be here after you've had your shower."

Soon the men are removing trousers and shirts, jackets and shoes, folding their filthy clothes and placing them neatly on the benches.

Lale is cheered at the prospect of water but knows he will probably not see his clothes again, nor the money inside them.

He takes off his clothes and places them on the bench, but outrage threatens to overwhelm him. From his trouser pocket he removes a slim packet of matches, a reminder of past pleasures, and steals a glance at the nearest officer. The man is looking away. Lale strikes a match. This might be the final act of his own free will. He holds the match to the lining of his jacket, covers it with his trousers, and hurries to join the line of men at the showers. Behind him, within seconds, he hears screams of "Fire!" Lale looks back, sees naked men pushing and shoving to get away as an SS officer attempts to beat out the flames.

He hasn't yet reached the showers but finds himself shivering. *What have I done?* He's just spent several days telling everyone around him to keep their heads down, do as they're told, don't antagonize anyone, and now he's gone and lit a fire inside a building. He has little doubt what would happen if someone pointed him out as the arsonist. *Stupid. Stupid.*

In the shower block, he settles himself, breathes deeply. Hundreds of shivering men stand shoulder to shoulder as cold water rains down on them. They tilt their heads back and drink it in desperately, despite its rankness. Many try to lessen their embarrassment by covering their genitals with their hands. Lale washes the sweat, grime, and stink from his body and hair. Water hisses through the pipes and hammers the floor. When it ceases, the doors to the changing room reopen, and without command they walk back to see what has replaced their clothes—old Russian army uniforms and boots.

"Before you dress, you must visit the barber," a smirking SS officer tells the men. "Outside—hurry."

Once again, the men fall into lines. They move toward the prisoner standing ready with a razor. When it is Lale's turn, he sits on the chair with his back straight and his head held high. He watches the SS officers walk the length of the line, assaulting the naked prisoners with the ends of their weapons, offering insults and cruel laughter. Lale sits straighter and lifts his head higher as the hair on his head is reduced to stubble, not flinching when the razor nicks his scalp.

A shove in the back by an officer indicates that he is done. He follows the line back into the changing room, where he joins the search for clothing and wooden shoes of the right size. What is there is dirty and stained, but he manages to find shoes that more or less fit and hopes the Russian clothes he grabs will do. Once dressed, he leaves the building as instructed.

It is getting dark. He walks through the rain, one of countless men, for what seems like a long time. The thickening mud makes it difficult for him to lift his feet. But he trudges on determinedly. Some men struggle or fall to their hands and knees and are beaten until they get back up. If they do not, they are shot.

Lale tries to separate the heavy, sodden uniform from his skin. It rubs and chafes, and the smell of wet wool and dirt brings him back to the cattle train. Lale looks to the heavens, trying to swallow as much rain as he can. The sweet taste is the best thing he's had in days, the only thing he's had in days, his thirst compounding his weakness, blurring his vision. He gulps it down. Cupping his hands, he slurps wildly. In the distance he sees spotlights surrounding a vast area. His semidelirious state makes them seem like beacons, sparkling, dancing in the rain, showing him the way home. Calling, *Come to me. I will provide shelter, warmth, and nourishment. Keep walking.* But as he walks through gates, this time bearing no message, offering no deal, no promise of freedom in exchange for toil, Lale realizes the sparkling mirage has gone. He's in another prison.

Beyond this yard, disappearing into the darkness, is another compound. The tops of the fences are lined with razor wire. Lale sees SS up in the lookouts pointing rifles in his direction. Lightning hits a fence nearby. *They are electrified.* The thunder is not loud enough to drown out the sound of a shot, another man falling.

"We made it."

Lale turns to see Aron pushing his way toward him. Drenched, bedraggled. But alive.

"Yeah, looks like we're home. You look a sight."

"You haven't seen yourself. Consider me a mirror."

"No thanks."

"What happens now?" says Aron, sounding like a child.

❧

GOING WITH THE STEADY FLOW OF MEN, THEY EACH SHOW their tattooed arm to an SS officer standing outside a building, who records the number on a clipboard. After a forceful shove in the back, Lale and Aron find themselves in Block 7, a large hut with triple bunks down one wall. Dozens of men are forced into the building. They scramble and shove each other out of the way to lay claim to a space. If they are lucky or aggressive enough, they might share with only one or two others. Luck isn't on Lale's side. He and Aron climb up onto a top-level bunk already occupied by two other prisoners. They've had no food for days and there isn't much fight left in them. As best he can, Lale curls up on the straw-filled sack that passes for a mattress. He pushes his hands against his stomach in an attempt to quell the cramps invading his guts. Several men call out to their guards, "We need food."

The reply comes back: "You'll get something in the morning."

"We'll all be dead from starvation by morning," says someone in the back of the block.

"And at peace," a hollow voice adds.

"These mattresses have hay in them," someone else says. "Maybe we should continue to act like cattle and eat that."

Snatches of quiet laughter. No response from the officer.

And then, from deep in the dormitory, a hesitant "Mooooooo . . ."

Laughter. Quiet, but real. The officer, present but invisible, doesn't interrupt, and eventually the men fall asleep, stomachs rumbling.

IT'S STILL DARK WHEN LALE WAKES, NEEDING TO TAKE A PISS. He scrambles over his sleeping companions, down to the floor, and feels his way to the back of the block, thinking it might be the safest place to relieve himself. Approaching, he hears voices: Slovak and German. He is relieved to see that there are facilities, albeit crude, for them to shit. Long ditches run behind the building, with planks of wood placed over them. Three prisoners are sitting across the ditch, shitting and talking quietly to each other. From the other end of the building, Lale sees two SS approaching in the semidarkness, smoking, laughing, their rifles hung loosely down their backs. The flickering perimeter floodlights make disturbing shadows of them, and Lale can't make out what they are saying. His bladder is full, but he hesitates.

In unison, the officers flick their cigarettes up into the air, whip their rifles around, and open fire. The bodies of the three who were taking a shit are thrown back into the ditch. Lale's breath catches in his throat. He presses his back against the building as the officers pass him. He catches the profile of one of them—a boy, just a kid.

As they disappear into the darkness, Lale makes a vow to himself: *I will live to leave this place. I will walk out a free man. If there is a hell, I will see these murderers burn in it.* He thinks of his family back in Krompachy and hopes that his presence here is at least saving them from a similar fate.

Lale relieves himself and returns to his bunk.

"The shots," says Aron, "what were they?"

"I didn't see."

Aron swings his leg over Lale on his way to the ground.

"Where are you going?"

"A piss."

Lale reaches to the side of the bed, clutches Aron's hand. "Hold on."

"Why?"

"You heard the shots," says Lale. "Just hold on until the morning."

Aron says nothing as he clambers back into bed and lies down, his two fists curled against his crotch in fear and defiance.

⁂

HIS FATHER HAD BEEN PICKING UP A CUSTOMER FROM THE train station. Mr. Sheinberg prepared to lift himself elegantly into the carriage as Lale's father placed his fine leather luggage on the seat opposite. Where had he traveled from? Prague? Bratislava? Vienna, perhaps? Wearing a fine woolen suit, his shoes freshly shined, he smiled and spoke briefly to Lale's father as he climbed up front. His father encouraged the horse to move on. Like most of the other men Lale's father ferried around with his taxi service, Mr. Sheinberg was returning home from important business. Lale wanted to be like him rather than like his father.

Mr. Sheinberg did not have his wife with him that day. Lale loved to glimpse Mrs. Sheinberg and the other women who traveled in his father's carriages, their small hands encased in white gloves, their elegant pearl earrings matching their necklaces. He loved the beautiful women in fine clothing and jewels who sometimes accompanied the important men. The only advantage of helping his father came from opening the carriage door for them, taking their hand as he assisted them down, inhaling their scent, dreaming of the lives they led.

2

"Outside. Everyone outside!"

Whistles blow and dogs bark. Sunlight from a clear morning streams through the door into Block 7. The men disentangle themselves from each other, climb down from their bunks, and shuffle outside. They stand around just outside the building. No one is prepared to move too far away. They wait. And wait. Those who were shouting and blowing whistles have disappeared. The men shuffle their feet back and forth, whisper to the person nearest them. Looking over at other blocks, they see the same scene being played out. What now? Wait.

Eventually, an SS officer and a prisoner approach Block 7, which falls silent. No introductions are made. The prisoner calls out numbers from a clipboard. The SS officer stands alongside, tapping his foot impatiently, slapping his thigh with his swagger stick. It takes a moment for the prisoners to realize that the numbers relate to the tattoos they each bear on their left arm. When the roll call is over, two numbers have received no response.

"You"—the roll caller points to a man on the end of the row—"go back inside and see if anyone is still there."

The man looks at him with questioning eyes. He hasn't understood a word. The man beside him whispers the instructions and he hurries inside. A few moments later he returns, holds up his right hand, and extends his index and middle finger: two dead.

The SS officer steps forward. He speaks in German. The prisoners have learned, already, to keep their mouths shut and stand obediently waiting, hoping someone among them will be able to translate. Lale gets it all.

"You will have two meals a day. One in the morning and one in the evening. If you survive until evening." He pauses, a grim smile on his face. "After your morning meal, you will work until we tell you to stop. You will continue with the construction of this camp. We have many more people to transport here." His smile becomes a proud grin. "Follow the instructions of your kapo and those in charge of the building program and you will see the sun go down."

There is a sound of clanging metal, and the prisoners turn to see a group of men approaching, carrying two cauldrons and armfuls of small metal tins. Breakfast. A few prisoners start to head toward the smaller group, as though to offer assistance.

"If anyone moves they will be shot," barks the SS officer, raising his rifle. "There will be no second chances."

The officer leaves, and the prisoner who conducted the roll call addresses the group. "You heard him," says the man in Polish-accented German. "I am your kapo, your boss. You will form two lines to get your food. Anyone who complains will suffer consequences."

The men jockey into line and several start whispering among

themselves, asking if anyone has understood what "the German" said. Lale tells those nearest to him and asks them to pass it along. He will translate as much as he can.

As he reaches the front of the line he gratefully accepts a small tin cup, its contents slopping over the rough hands that thrust it at him. He steps aside and examines his meal. It is brown, contains nothing solid, and has a smell he cannot identify. It is neither tea nor coffee nor soup. He fears he will bring the foul liquid back up if he drinks it slowly. So he closes his eyes, pinches his nostrils with his fingers, and gulps it down. Others are not so successful.

Aron, standing nearby, raises his cup in a mock toast. "I got a piece of potato, what about you?"

"Best meal I've had in ages."

"Are you always so upbeat?"

"Ask me again at the end of the day," Lale says with a wink. Returning his empty cup to the prisoner who handed it to him, Lale thanks him with a quick nod and half a smile.

The kapo shouts, "When you lazy bastards have finished your dining, get back into line! You have work to do!"

Lale passes on the instruction.

"You'll follow me," the kapo shouts, "and you'll follow the instructions of the foreman. Any slacking off, I'll know about it."

⁂

LALE AND THE OTHERS FIND THEMSELVES IN FRONT OF A PARtially erected building, a replica of their own block. Other prisoners are already there: carpenters and bricklayers all quietly laboring in the established rhythm of people used to working together.

"You. Yes, you. Get up on the roof. You can work up there."

The command is directed at Lale. Looking around, he spies a

ladder going up to the roof. Two prisoners squat there, waiting to receive the tiles that are being shuttled up to them. The two men move aside as Lale clambers up. The roof consists only of wooden beams for supporting the tiles.

"Be careful," one of the workmen warns him. "Move farther up the roofline and watch us. It's not difficult—you'll soon get the hang of it." The man is Russian.

"My name's Lale."

"Introductions later, OK?" The two men exchange a look. "You understand me?"

"Yes," Lale replies in Russian. The men smile.

Lale watches as they receive the heavy clay tiles from the pair of hands poking over the lip of the roof, crawl to where the last tiles were laid, and carefully overlap them before moving back to the ladder for the next ones. The Russian had been correct—it's not difficult work—and it isn't long before Lale joins them in accepting and laying the tiles. On the warm spring day, only the hunger pains and cramps prevent him from matching the more experienced workers.

A few hours pass before they are permitted to take a break. Lale heads for the ladder but the Russian stops him.

"It's safer to stay up here and rest. You can't be seen well this high up."

Lale follows the men, who clearly know the best place to sit and stretch out: the corner, where stronger timber was used to reinforce the roof.

"How long have you been here?" Lale asks as soon as they settle down.

"About two months, I think. Hard to tell after a while."

"Where did you come from? I mean, how did you end up here? Are you Jewish?"

"One question at a time." The Russian chuckles and the younger, larger worker rolls his eyes at the ignorance of the newcomer, yet to learn his place in the camp.

"We're not Jewish, we are Russian soldiers. We got separated from our unit, and the fucking Germans caught us and put us to work. What about you? A Jew?"

"Yes. I'm part of a large group brought in yesterday from Slovakia—all Jews."

The Russians exchange a glance. The older man turns away, closing his eyes, raising his face to the sun, leaving it to his companion to continue the conversation.

"Look around. You can see from up here how many blocks are being built and how much land they keep clearing."

Lale pushes himself onto his elbows and observes the vast area contained within the electrified fence. Blocks like the one he is helping construct stretch out into the distance. He experiences a jolt of horror at what this place might become. He wrestles with what to say next, not wanting to give voice to his distress. He settles back down, turning his head away from his companions, desperate to bring his emotions under control. He must trust no one, reveal little about himself, be cautious . . .

The man watches him closely. He says, "I've heard the SS boasting that this is going to be the biggest concentration camp of all."

"Is that right?" says Lale, forcing his voice above a whisper. "Well, if we're going to build it together, you might as well tell me your name."

"Andor," he says. "And this big oaf with me is Boris. He doesn't say much."

"Talking can get you killed here," Boris mutters as he stretches his hand out to Lale.

"What else can you tell me about the people here?" asks Lale. "And who the hell are these kapos?"

"You tell him," says Boris, yawning.

"Well, there are other Russian soldiers like us, but not many, and then there are all the different triangles."

"Like the green triangle my kapo wears?" Lale says.

Andor laughs. "Oh, the greens are the worst—they're criminals: killers, rapists, that kind of man. They make good guards because they're terrible people." He continues, "Others are here because of their anti-German political views. They wear a red triangle. You'll see a few, not many, with a black triangle—they are lazy bastards and they don't last long. And finally, there are you and your friends."

"We wear the yellow star."

"Yes, you wear the star. Your crime is to be Jewish."

"Why don't you have a color?" asks Lale.

Andor shrugs. "We're just the enemy."

Boris snorts. "They insult us by sharing our uniforms with the rest of you. They can't do much worse than that."

A whistle blows and the three men get back to work.

⸎

THAT NIGHT, THE MEN IN BLOCK 7 GATHER IN SMALL GROUPS, to talk, share what they've learned, and question. Several move to the far end of the hut, where they offer prayers to their god. These mingle into something unintelligible. *Are they praying for guidance, vengeance, acceptance?* It seems to Lale that without a rabbi to guide them, each man prays for what is most important to him. And he decides this is as it should be. He moves between the groups of men, listening but not taking part.

By the end of his first day Lale exhausted the knowledge of his two Russian coworkers. For the rest of the week he heeds his own advice: keeps his head down, does what he is asked, never argues. At the same time, he observes everyone and everything going on around him. It is clear to him, looking at the design of the new buildings, that the Germans lack any architectural intelligence. Whenever possible, he listens to the talk and gossip of the SS, who don't know he understands them. They give him ammunition of the only sort available to him—knowledge, to be stored up for later. The SS stand around most of the day, leaning against walls, smoking, keeping only one eye on things. By eavesdropping, he learns that Commandant Hoess is a lazy bastard who hardly ever shows his face, and that accommodations for the Germans at Auschwitz are superior to those at Birkenau, which has no access to cigarettes or beer.

One group of workers stands out to Lale. They keep to themselves, wear civilian clothes, and speak to the SS without fearing for their safety. Lale is determined to find out who these men are. Other prisoners never pick up a piece of wood or tile but instead walk casually around the compound on other business. His kapo is one such. *How to get a job like that?* Such a position would offer the best chance to find out what is going on in the camp, what the plans are for Birkenau and, more important, for him.

Lale is on the roof, tiling in the sun, when he spies his kapo heading in their direction. "Come on, you lazy bastards, work faster," Lale yells. "We've got a block to finish!"

He continues barking orders as the kapo appears below. Lale has made a habit of acknowledging him with a deferential nod of the head. On one occasion he received a short nod back. He has spoken to him in Polish. At the very least, his kapo has accepted him as a subservient prisoner who will not cause problems.

With a half smile, the kapo makes eye contact with Lale and beckons him down from the roof. Lale approaches him with his head bowed.

"Do you like what you're doing, on the roof?" asks the kapo.

"I'll do whatever I'm told to do," replies Lale.

"But everyone wants an easier life, yes?"

Lale says nothing.

"I need a boy," the kapo says, playing with the fraying edge of his Russian army shirt. It's too big for him, chosen to make the little man appear larger and more powerful than those he must control. From his gap-toothed mouth Lale experiences the pungent smell of partially digested meat.

"You will do whatever I ask you to. Bring me my food, clean my boots, and be beside me whenever I want you. Do this, and I can make life easier for you; fail me, and there will be consequences."

Lale stands beside his kapo as his answer to the job offer, wondering if by moving from builder to lackey he is making a deal with the devil.

⌖

ON A BEAUTIFUL SPRING DAY, NOT TOO HOT, LALE WATCHES AS a large, enclosed truck continues past the usual point for unloading building supplies. It drives around the back of the administration building. Lale knows that the boundary fence lies not far beyond and he has never dared venture to this area, but curiosity gets the better of him now. He walks after it with an air of "I belong here, I can go where I want."

He peers around the corner at the back of the building. The truck pulls up beside an odd bus that has been adapted into a bunker of sorts, with steel plates nailed across the window frames. Lale watches as dozens of naked men are herded out of the truck and led toward the bus. Some enter willingly. Those who resist are hit with a rifle butt. Fellow prisoners drag the semiconscious objectors to their fate.

The bus is so full that the last men to board cling to the steps with their tiptoes, their naked bottoms hanging out the door. Officers shove their weight against the bodies. Then the doors are slammed shut. One officer walks around the bus, rapping on the metal sheets, checking that everything is secure. A nimble officer clambers onto the roof with a canister in his hand. Unable to move, Lale watches as he opens a small hatch on the roof of the bus and upends the canister. Then he slams the lid down and latches it. As the guard scurries down, the bus shakes violently and muffled screams can be heard.

Lale drops to his knees, retching. He remains there, sick in the dirt, as the screams fade.

When the bus is still and quiet, the doors are opened. Dead men fall out like blocks of stone.

A group of prisoners is marched out from beyond the other corner of the building. The truck backs up and the prisoners begin transferring the bodies onto it, staggering under the weight while trying to hide their distress. Lale has witnessed an unimaginable act. He staggers to his feet, standing on the threshold of hell, an inferno of feelings raging inside him.

The next morning he cannot get up. He is burning up.

～

IT TAKES SEVEN DAYS FOR LALE TO REGAIN CONSCIOUSNESS. Someone is pouring water gently into his mouth. He registers a cool, damp rag on his forehead.

"There, boy," says a voice. "Take it easy."

Lale opens his eyes to see a stranger, an older man, peering gently into his face. He pushes himself up onto his elbows, and the stranger supports him as he sits up. He looks around, confused. What day is it? Where is he?

"The fresh air might do you good," says the man, taking Lale's elbow.

He is escorted outside into a cloudless day, and he shivers at the memory of the last day like this. His world spins and he staggers. The stranger supports him, leading him to a nearby pile of timber.

Pulling up Lale's sleeve, he points to the tattooed number.

"My name is Pepan. I am the *Tätowierer*. What do you think of my handiwork?"

"Tätowierer?" asks Lale. "You mean, you did this to me?"

Pepan shrugs, looking Lale directly in the eye. "I wasn't given a choice."

Lale shakes his head. "This number wouldn't have been my first choice of tattoo."

"What would you have preferred?" asks Pepan.

Lale smiles slyly.

"What's her name?"

"My sweetheart? I don't know. We haven't met yet."

Pepan chuckles. The two men sit in companionable silence. Lale traces a finger over his numbers.

"What is your accent?" asks Lale.

"I am French."

"And what happened to me?" Lale asks finally.

"Typhus. You were destined for an early grave."

Lale shudders. "Then why am I sitting here with you?"

"I was walking past your block just as your body was being thrown onto a cart for the dead and dying. A young man was pleading with the SS to leave you, saying that he would take care of you. When they went into the next block he pushed you off the cart and started dragging you back inside. I went and helped him."

"How long ago was this?"

"Seven, eight days. Since then the men in your block have looked after you during the night. I've spent as much time as I can during the day caring for you. How do you feel?"

"I feel OK. I don't know what to say, how to thank you."

"Thank the man who pushed you from the cart. It was his courage that held you back from the jaws of death."

"I will when I find out who it was. Do you know?"

"No. I'm sorry. We didn't exchange names."

Lale closes his eyes for a few moments, letting the sun warm his skin, giving him the energy, the will, to go on. He lifts his sagging shoulders, and resolve seeps back into him. He is still alive. He stands on shaking legs, stretching, trying to breathe new life back into an ailing body in need of rest, nourishment, and hydration.

"Sit down, you're still very weak."

Conceding the obvious, Lale does so. Only now his back is straighter, his voice firmer. He gives Pepan a smile. The old Lale is back, almost as hungry for information as he is for food. "I see you wear a red star," he says.

"Ah, yes. I was an academic in Paris and was too outspoken for my own good."

"What did you teach?"

"Economics."

"And being a teacher of economics got you here? How?"

"Well, Lale, a man who lectures on taxation and interest rates can't help but get involved in the politics of his country. Politics will help you understand the world until you don't understand it anymore, and then it will get you thrown into a prison camp. Politics and religion both."

"And will you go back to that life when you leave here?"

"An optimist! I don't know what my future holds, or yours."

Through the noise of construction, dogs barking, and guards shouting, Pepan leans forward and asks, "Are you as strong in character as you are physically?"

Lale returns Pepan's gaze. "I'm a survivor."

"Your strength can be a weakness, given the circumstances we find ourselves in. Charm and an easy smile will get you in trouble."

"I am a survivor."

"Well, then maybe I can help you survive in here."

"You have friends in high places?"

Pepan laughs and slaps Lale on the back. "No. No friends in high places. Like I told you, I am the Tätowierer. And I have been told that the number of people coming here will be increasing very soon."

They sit with the thought for a moment. What lodges in Lale's mind is that somewhere, someone is making decisions, plucking numbers from—where? *How do you decide who comes here? What information do you base those decisions on? Race, religion, or politics?*

"You intrigue me, Lale. I was drawn to you. You had a strength that even your sick body couldn't hide. It brought you to this point, sitting in front of me today."

Lale hears the words but struggles with what Pepan is saying. They are sitting in a place where people are dying every day, every hour, every minute.

"Would you like a job working with me?" Pepan brings Lale back from the bleakness. "Or are you happy doing whatever they have you doing?"

"I do what I can to survive."

"Then take my job offer."

"You want me to tattoo other men?"

"Someone has to do it."

"I don't think I could do that. Scar someone, hurt someone—it does hurt, you know."

Pepan pulls back his sleeve to reveal his own number. "It hurts like hell. If you don't take the job, someone will who has less soul than you do, and he will hurt these people more."

"Working for the kapo is not the same as defiling hundreds of innocent people."

A long silence follows. Lale again enters his dark place. *Do those making the decisions have a family, a wife, children, parents? They can't possibly.*

"You can tell yourself that, but you are still a Nazi puppet. Whether it is with me or the kapo, or building blocks, you are still doing their dirty work."

"You have a way of putting things."

"So?"

"Then yes. If you can arrange it, I will work for you."

"Not for me. With me. But you must work quickly and efficiently and not make trouble with the SS."

"OK."

Pepan stands, goes to walk away. Lale grabs at his shirtsleeve.

"Pepan, why have you chosen me?"

"I saw a half-starved young man risk his life to save you. I figure you must be someone worth saving. I'll come for you tomorrow morning. Get some rest now."

THAT NIGHT AS HIS BLOCKMATES RETURN, LALE NOTICES THAT Aron is missing. He asks the two others sharing his bed what has happened to him, how long he's been gone.

"About a week," comes the reply.

Lale's stomach drops.

"The kapo couldn't find you," the man says. "Aron could have told him you were ill, but he feared the kapo would add you to the death cart again if he knew, so he said you were already gone."

"And the kapo discovered the truth?"

"No," yawns the man, exhausted from work. "But he was so pissed off, he took Aron anyway."

Lale struggles to contain his tears.

The second bunkmate rolls onto his elbow. "You put big ideas into his head. He wanted to save 'the one.'"

"To save one is to save the world," Lale completes the phrase.

The men sink into silence for a while. Lale looks at the ceiling, blinks away tears. Aron is not the first person to die here and will not be the last.

"Thank you," he says.

"We tried to continue what Aron started, to see if we could save the one."

"We took turns," a young boy says from below, "smuggling

water and sharing our bread with you, forcing it down your throat."

Another picks up the story. He rises from the bunk below, haggard, with cloudy blue eyes, his voice flat but still full of the need to tell his part of the story. "We changed your soiled clothes. We swapped them with someone's who had died overnight."

Lale is now unable to stop the tears that roll down his emaciated cheeks.

"I can't . . ."

He can't do anything but be appreciative. He knows he has a debt he cannot repay, not now, not here, realistically not ever.

He falls asleep to the soulful sound of Hebrew chants from those who still cling to faith.

THE NEXT MORNING LALE IS IN THE LINE FOR BREAKFAST when Pepan appears by his side, takes his arm quietly, and steers him away toward the main compound. There, the trucks unload their human cargo. He feels as though he has wandered into a scene from a classical tragedy. Some of the actors are the same, most are new, their lines unwritten, their role not yet determined. His life experience has not equipped him to understand what is happening. But he remembers being here before. *Not as an observer but a participant. What will my role be now?* He closes his eyes and imagines he is facing another version of himself, looking at his left arm. It is unnumbered. Opening his eyes again, he looks down at the tattoo on his real left arm, then back to the scene in front of him.

He takes in the hundreds of new prisoners who are gathered there. Boys, young men, terror etched on each of their faces. Holding on to each other. Hugging themselves. SS and dogs shepherd them like lambs to the slaughter. They obey. Whether they live or die this day is about to be decided. Lale stops following Pepan and stands frozen. Pepan doubles back and guides him to some small tables with tattooing equipment. Those who have passed selection are guided into a line in front of their table. They will be marked. Other new arrivals—the old, infirm, no skills identified—are walking dead.

A shot rings out. Men flinch. Someone falls. Lale looks in the direction of the shot only for Pepan to grab his face and twist his head away.

A group of SS, mostly young, walk toward Pepan and Lale, guarding an older SS officer. Mid- to late forties, straight-backed in his immaculate uniform, his cap sitting precisely on his head—*a perfect mannequin*, thinks Lale, like those he occasionally helped dress when he worked in the department store in Bratislava.

The SS stop in front of them. Pepan steps forward, acknowledging the officer with a bowed head as Lale watches.

"Oberscharführer Houstek, I have enlisted this prisoner to help." Pepan indicates Lale standing behind him.

Houstek turns to Lale.

Pepan continues. "I believe he will learn fast."

Houstek, steely eyed, glares at Lale before wagging a finger for him to step forward. Lale does so.

"What languages do you speak?"

"Slovak, German, Russian, French, Hungarian, and a little Polish," Lale answers, looking him in the eye.

"Humph." Houstek walks away.

Lale leans over and whispers to Pepan, "A man of few words. I take it I got the job?"

Pepan turns on Lale, fire in his eyes and his voice, though he speaks quietly. "Do not underestimate him. Lose your bravado, or you will lose your life. Next time you talk to him, do not raise your eyes above the level of his boots."

"I'm sorry," Lale says. "I won't."

When will I learn?

3

July 1942

Lale is slowly waking, holding on to a dream that has put a smile on his face. *Stay, stay, let me stay here just a moment longer, please . . .*

While Lale likes meeting all kinds of people, he particularly likes meeting women. He thinks them all beautiful, regardless of their age, their appearance, how they are dressed. The highlight of his daily routine is walking through the women's department, where he works. That's when he flirts with the young and not-so-young women who work behind the counter.

Lale hears the main doors to the department store open. He looks up, and a woman hurries inside. Behind her, two Slovak soldiers stand in the doorway and don't follow her in. He hurries over to her with a reassuring smile. "You're OK," he says. "You're safe here with me." She accepts his hand and he leads her toward a counter full of extravagant bottles of perfume. Looking at several, he settles on one and holds it toward her. She turns her neck in a playful manner. Lale softly sprays first one side of her neck and then the other. Their eyes meet as her head turns. Both wrists are held out, and each receives its reward. She brings one wrist to her nose, closes her eyes, and sniffs lightly. The same wrist is offered to Lale. Gently holding her hand, he brings it close to his face as he bends and inhales the intoxicating mix of perfume and youth.

"Yes. That's the one for you," Lale says.

"I'll take it."

Lale hands the bottle over to the waiting shop assistant, who begins to wrap it.

"Is there anything else I can help you with?" he says.

Faces flash before him, smiling young women dance around him, happy, living life to the fullest. Lale holds the arm of the young lady he met in the women's department. His dream seems to rush ahead. Lale and the lady walk into an exquisite restaurant, dimly lit by a few wall sconces. On every table, a flickering candle holds down the heavy jacquard tablecloth. Expensive jewelry projects colors onto the walls. The noise of silver cutlery on fine china is softened by the dulcet sounds of the string quartet silhouetted in one corner. The concierge greets him warmly as he takes the coat from Lale's companion and steers them toward a table. As they sit, the maître d' shows Lale a bottle of wine. Without taking his eyes from his companion, he nods and the bottle is uncorked and poured. Both Lale and the lady feel for their glass. Their eyes still locked, they raise their hands and sip. Lale's dream jumps forward again. He is close to waking up. *No.* Now he is riffling through his wardrobe, selecting a suit, a shirt, considering and rejecting ties until he finds the right one and attaches it perfectly. He slides polished shoes onto his feet. From the bedside table he pockets his keys and wallet before bending down and pushing a wayward strand of hair from the face of his sleeping companion and lightly kissing her on the forehead. She stirs and smiles. In a husky voice she says, "Tonight . . ."

～

GUNSHOTS OUTSIDE CATAPULT LALE INTO WAKEFULNESS. HE is jostled by his bunkmates as they look for the threat. With the memory of her warm body still lingering, Lale rises slowly and is the last to line up for roll call. The prisoner beside him nudges him when he fails to respond to his number being called.

"What's wrong?"

"Nothing . . . everything. This place."

"It's the same as it was yesterday. And it will be the same to-morrow. You taught me that. What's changed for you?"

"You're right—same, same. It's just that, well, I had a dream about a girl I once knew, in another lifetime."

"What was her name?"

"I can't remember. It doesn't matter."

"You weren't in love with her, then?"

"I loved them all, but somehow none of them ever captured my heart. Does that make sense?"

"Not really. I'd settle for one girl to love and spend the rest of my life with."

～

IT HAS BEEN RAINING FOR DAYS, BUT THIS MORNING THE SUN threatens to shine a little light on the bleak Birkenau compound as Lale and Pepan prepare their work area. They have two tables, bottles of ink, plenty of needles.

"Get ready, Lale, here they come."

Lale looks up and is stunned at the sight of dozens of young women being escorted their way. He knew there were girls in Auschwitz, but not here, not in Birkenau, this hell of hells.

"Something a bit different today, Lale—they've moved some girls from Auschwitz to here, and some of them need their numbers redone."

"What?"

"Their numbers, they were made with a stamp, which was inefficient. We need to do them properly. No time to admire them, Lale—just do your job."

"I can't."

"Do your job, Lale. Don't say a word to any of them. Don't do anything stupid."

The row of young girls snakes back beyond his vision.

"I can't do this. Please, Pepan, we can't do this."

"Yes, you can, Lale. You must. If you don't, someone else will, and my saving you will have been for nothing. Just do the job, Lale." Pepan holds Lale's stare. Dread settles deep in Lale's bones. Pepan is right. He either follows the rules or risks death.

Lale starts the "job." He tries not to look up. He reaches out to take the piece of paper being handed to him. He must transfer the five digits onto the girl who held it. There is already a number there, but it has faded. He pushes the needle into her left arm, making a three, trying to be gentle. Blood oozes. But the needle hasn't gone deep enough, and he has to trace the number again. She doesn't flinch at the pain Lale knows he's inflicting. *They've been warned—say nothing, do nothing.* He wipes away the blood and rubs green ink into the wound.

"Hurry up!" Pepan whispers.

Lale is taking too long. Tattooing the arms of men is one thing; defiling the bodies of young girls is horrifying. Glancing up, Lale sees a man in a white coat slowly walking up the row of girls. Every now and then he stops to inspect the face and body of a terrified young woman. Eventually he reaches Lale. While Lale holds the arm of the girl in front of him as gently as he can, the man takes her face in his hand and turns it roughly this way and that. Lale looks up into the frightened eyes. Her lips move in readiness to speak. Lale squeezes her arm tightly to stop her. She looks at him and he mouths, "*Shh*." The man in the white coat releases her face and walks away.

"Well done," he whispers as he sets about tattooing the remaining four digits—4 9 0 2. When he has finished, he holds on to her arm for a moment longer than necessary, looking again into her eyes. He forces a small smile. She returns a smaller one. Her eyes, however, dance before him. As he looks into them, his heart seems simultaneously to stop and to begin beating for the first time, pounding, almost threatening to burst out of his chest. He looks down at the ground and it sways beneath him. Another piece of paper is thrust at him.

"Hurry up, Lale!" Pepan whispers urgently.

When he looks up again, she is gone.

⟩⟨

SEVERAL WEEKS LATER, LALE REPORTS FOR WORK AS USUAL. His table and equipment are already laid out and he looks around anxiously for Pepan. Lots of men are heading his way. He is startled by the approach of Oberscharführer Houstek, accompanied by a young SS officer. Lale bows his head and remembers Pepan's words: *Do not underestimate him.*

"You will be working alone today," Houstek mumbles.

As Houstek turns to walk away, Lale asks quietly, "Where is Pepan?"

Houstek stops, turns, and glares back at him. Lale's heart skips a beat.

"You are the Tätowierer now." Houstek turns to the SS officer. "And you are responsible for him."

As Houstek walks away, the SS officer puts his rifle to his shoulder and points it at Lale. Lale returns his stare, looking into the black eyes of a scrawny kid wearing a cruel smirk. Eventually Lale drops his gaze. *Pepan, you said this job might help save my life. But what has happened to you?*

"It seems my fate is in your hands," snarls the officer. "What do you think about that?"

"I'll try not to let you down."

"Try? You'll do better than try. You *will not* let me down."

"Yes, sir."

"What block are you in?"

"Number seven."

"When you're finished here, I'll show you to your room in one of the new blocks. You'll stay there from now on."

"I'm happy in my block, sir."

"Don't be stupid. You'll need protection now that you're the Tätowierer. You now work for the political wing of the SS—shit, maybe *I* should be scared of *you*." There is the smirk again.

Having survived this round of questioning, Lale pushes his luck.

"The process will go much faster, you know, if I have an assistant."

The SS officer takes a step closer to Lale, looking him up and down with contempt.

"What?"

"If you get someone to help me, the process will go faster and your boss will be happy."

As if instructed by Houstek, the officer turns away and walks down the line of young men waiting to be numbered, all of whom, bar one, have their heads bowed. Lale fears for the one staring back at the officer and is surprised when he is dragged by the arm and marched up to Lale.

"Your assistant. Do his number first."

Lale takes the piece of paper from the young man and quickly tattoos his arm.

"What's your name?" he asks.

"Leon."

"Leon, I am Lale, the Tätowierer," he says, his voice firm like Pepan's. "Now, stand beside me and watch what I'm doing. Starting tomorrow, you will work for me as my assistant. It just might save your life."

⌇

THE SUN HAS SET BY THE TIME THE LAST PRISONER HAS BEEN tattooed and shoved toward his new home. Lale's guard, whose name, he has found out, is Baretski, never wandered more than a few feet from him. He approaches Lale and his new assistant.

"Take him to your block, then come back here."

Lale hurries Leon to Block 7.

"Wait outside the block in the morning and I'll come and get you. If your kapo wants to know why you aren't going with the others to build, tell him you now work for the Tätowierer."

⌇

WHEN LALE RETURNS TO HIS WORKSTATION, HIS TOOLS HAVE been packed into a briefcase and his table has been folded. Baretski stands waiting for him.

"Bring these to your new room. Each morning, report to the administration building for supplies and to get instructions on where you will be working that day."

"Can I get an extra table and supplies for Leon?"

"Who?"

"My assistant."

"Just ask at administration for whatever you need."

He leads Lale to an area of the camp that is still under construction. Many of the buildings are unfinished, and the eerie quiet makes Lale shiver. One of these new blocks is complete, and Baretski shows Lale to a single room located immediately inside the door.

"You will sleep here," Baretski says. Lale puts his bag of tools on the hard floor and takes in the small, isolated room. He misses his friends in Block 7 already.

Next, following Baretski, Lale learns that he will now take his meals in an area near the administration building. In his role as Tätowierer, he will receive extra rations. They head to dinner while Baretski explains, "We want our workers to have their strength." He motions for Lale to take a spot in the dinner line. "Make the most of it."

As Baretski walks away, a ladle of weak soup and a chunk of bread are handed to Lale. He gulps them both down and is about to walk away.

"You may have more if you wish," says a plaintive voice.

Lale takes a second helping of bread, looking at the prisoners around him who eat in silence, sharing no pleasantries, only surreptitious glances. The feelings of mistrust and fear are obvious. Walking away, the bread shoved up his sleeve, he heads to his old home, Block 7. As he enters he nods to the kapo, who seems to have gotten the message that Lale is no longer his to command.

Going inside, Lale acknowledges the greetings of many of the men he has shared a block with, shared his fears and dreams of another life with. When he arrives at his old bunk, Leon is sitting there with his feet dangling over the side. Lale looks at the young man's face. His wide blue eyes have a gentleness and honesty that he finds endearing.

"Come outside with me for a moment."

Leon jumps from the bunk and follows him. All eyes are on the two of them. Walking around the side of the block, Lale pulls the chunk of stale bread from his sleeve and offers it to Leon, who devours it. Only when it's finished does he thank him.

"I knew you would have missed supper. I get extra rations now. I will try to share them with you and the others when I can. Now go back inside. Tell them I dragged you out here to chew you out. And keep your head down. I'll see you in the morning."

"Don't you want them to know you can get extra rations?"

"No. Let me see how things play out. I can't help them all at once, and they don't need an extra reason to fight among themselves."

Lale watches Leon enter his old block with a mixture of feelings that he finds hard to articulate. *Should I be fearful, now that I am privileged? Why do I feel sad about leaving my old position in the camp, even though it offered me no protection?* He wanders into the shadows of the half-finished buildings. He is alone.

That night, Lale sleeps stretched out for the first time in months. No one to kick, no one to push him. In the luxury of his own bed, he feels like a king. And just like a king, he must now be wary of people's motives for befriending him or taking him into their confidence. *Are they jealous? Do they want my job? Do I run the risk of being wrongly accused of something?* He has seen the consequences of greed and mistrust here. Most people believe that if there are fewer men, there will be more food to go around. Food is currency. With it, you stay alive. You have the strength to do what is asked of you. You get to live another day. Without it, you weaken to the point that you don't care anymore. His new position adds to the complexity of surviving. He is sure that as he left his block and walked past the bunks of beaten men, he heard someone mutter the word "collaborator."

THE NEXT MORNING, LALE IS WAITING WITH LEON OUTSIDE the administration building when Baretski arrives and compliments him on being early. Lale is holding his briefcase, and his table is resting on the ground beside him. Baretski tells Leon to stay where he is and Lale to follow him inside. Lale looks around the large reception area. He can see corridors running off in different directions, with what look like offices adjoining. Behind the large reception desk are several rows of small desks with young women all working diligently—filing, transcribing. Baretski introduces him to an SS officer—"Meet the Tätowierer"—and tells him again to get his supplies and instructions here each day. Lale asks for an extra table and tools, as he has an assistant waiting outside. The request is granted without comment. Lale breathes a sigh of relief. He has saved one man from hard labor, at least. He thinks of Pepan and silently thanks him. He takes the table and stuffs the extra supplies into his bag. As Lale turns away, the administration clerk calls out to him.

"Carry that bag with you at all times and identify yourself with the words 'Politische Abteilung,' and no one will bother you. Return the numbered papers to us every night, but keep the bag."

Baretski snorts beside Lale. "It's true—with that bag and those words you are safe, except from me, of course. Screw up and get me into trouble, and no bag or words will save you." His hand goes to his pistol, rests on the holster, flicks the catch open. Closed. Open. Closed. His breathing grows deeper.

Lale does the smart thing: lowers his eyes and turns away.

⁓

TRANSPORTS COME INTO AUSCHWITZ-BIRKENAU AT ALL TIMES of day and night. It isn't unusual for Lale and Leon to work around the clock. On such days, Baretski shows his most unpleasant side. He screams abuse or beats Leon, blaming him for keeping him from his bed with his slowness. Lale quickly learns that the bad treatment **gets** worse if he tries to prevent it.

Finishing up in the early hours one morning at Auschwitz, Baretski turns to walk away before Lale and Leon have packed up. Then he turns back, a look of indecision on his face.

"Oh, fuck it—you two can walk back to Birkenau on your own. I'm sleeping here tonight. Just be back at eight in the morning."

"How are we supposed to know what time it is?" Lale asks.

"I don't give a fuck how you do it, just be here. And don't even think about running away. I'll hunt you down myself, kill you, and enjoy it." He staggers off.

"What do we do?" Leon asks.

"What the asshole told us. Come on—I'll get you up in time to make it back here."

"I'm so tired. Can't we stay here?"

"No. If you're not seen in your block in the morning, they'll go out looking for you. Come on, let's get going."

~

LALE RISES WITH THE SUN, AND HE AND LEON MAKE THE TWO-and-a-half-mile trek back to Auschwitz. They wait for what seems like an hour until Baretski shows up. It is obvious he didn't go straight to bed but stayed up drinking. When his breath is foul, his temper is worse.

"Get moving," he bellows.

With no sign of new prisoners, Lale has to reluctantly ask the question: "To where?"

"Back to Birkenau. The transports have dropped the latest batch there."

~

AS THE TRIO WALKS THE SEVERAL MILES BACK TO BIRKENAU, Leon stumbles and falls—fatigue and lack of nourishment overcoming him. He picks himself back up. Baretski slows his walk, seemingly waiting for Leon to catch up. As Leon does, Baretski sticks his leg out, causing him to fall again. Several times more on the journey, Baretski plays his little game. The walk and the pleasure he derives from tripping Leon seem to sober him up. Each time, he watches Lale for his reaction. He gets nothing.

On arriving back at Birkenau, Lale is surprised to see Houstek overseeing the selection of who will be sent to Lale and Leon to live another day. They begin their work while Baretski marches up and down the line of young men, trying to look competent in front of his superior. Exhausted, Leon is startled by the sound of squealing from the young man he is trying to tattoo. He drops his tattooing stick. As he bends down to pick it up, Baretski hits him on the back with his rifle, splaying him facedown in the dirt. He puts a foot on his back and presses him down.

"We can get the job done faster if you let him pick himself up and get on with it," Lale says, watching Leon breathe short and sharply beneath Baretski's boot.

Houstek bears down on the three men and mumbles something to Baretski. When Houstek disappears, Baretski, with a sour smile, pushes his foot down hard on Leon's body before releasing it.

"I am just a humble servant of the SS. You, Tätowierer, have been placed under the auspices of the political wing, which answers only to Berlin. It was your lucky day when the Frenchman introduced you to Houstek and you told him how clever you are, speaking all those languages."

There is no correct answer to this, so Lale busies himself with his work. A muddied Leon rises, coughing.

"So, Tätowierer," Baretski says, his sick smile returning, "how about we be friends?"

⁓

An advantage of being Tätowierer is that Lale knows the date. It is written on the papers he is given each morning and that he returns each evening. But it is not just the papers that tell him the date. Sunday is the only day of the week the other prisoners are not forced to work and can spend the day milling around in the compound or staying near their blocks, huddled together in small groups—friendships brought into the camp, friendships made in the camp.

It is a Sunday when he sees her. He recognizes her at once. They walk toward each other, Lale on his own, she with a group of girls, all with shaven heads, all wearing the same plain clothing. There is nothing to distinguish her except for those eyes. Black—no, brown. The darkest brown he'd ever seen. For the second time, they peer into each other's souls. Lale's heart skips a beat. The gaze lingers.

"Tätowierer!" Baretski places a hand on Lale's shoulder, breaking the spell.

The prisoners move away, not wanting to be near an SS officer or the prisoner to whom he is talking. The group of girls scatters, leaving her looking at Lale, he looking at her. Baretski's eyes move from one to the other as they stand in a perfect triangle, each waiting for the other to shift. Baretski has a knowing smile. Bravely, one of her friends advances and pulls her back into the group.

"Very nice," Baretski says as he and Lale walk away. Lale ignores him and fights to control the hatred he feels.

"Would you like to meet her?" Again, Lale refuses to respond.

"Write to her, tell her you like her."

How stupid does he think I am?

"I'll get you paper and a pencil and bring her your letter. What do you say? Do you know her name?"

34902.

Lale walks on. He knows that the penalty for a prisoner caught with a pen or paper is death.

"Where are we going?" Lale changes the subject.

"To Auschwitz. Herr Doktor needs more patients."

A chill runs through Lale. He remembers the man in the white coat, his hairy hands on that beautiful girl's face. Lale has never felt so uneasy about a doctor as he did that day.

"But it's Sunday."

Baretski laughs. "Oh, you think just because the others don't work on Sunday, you should get it off, too? Would you like to discuss this with Herr Doktor?" Baretski's laughter grows shrill, sending more shivers down Lale's spine. "Please do that for me, Tätowierer. Tell Herr Doktor it is your day off. I would so enjoy it."

Lale knows when to shut up. He strides off, putting some distance between himself and Baretski.

4

As they walk to Auschwitz, Baretski seems in a jovial mood and peppers Lale with questions. "How old are you?" "What did you do before—you know, before you were brought here?"

For the most part, Lale answers with questions, and he discovers that Baretski likes talking about himself. He learns that Baretski is only a year younger than Lale, but that is where the similarities end. He talks about women like a teenager. Lale decides he can make this difference work for him and begins telling Baretski of his winning ways with women, how it's all about respecting them and what they care about.

"Have you ever given a girl flowers?" asks Lale.

"No, why would I do that?"

"Because they like a man who gives them flowers. Better still if you pick them yourself."

"Well, I'm not gonna do that. I'd get laughed at."

"By who?"

"My friends."

"You mean other men?"

"Well, yeah—they'd think I was a sissy."

"And what do you think the girl getting the flowers would think?"

"What does it matter what she thinks?" He begins smirking and yanking at his groin. "That's all I want from them, and that's what they want from me. I know these things."

Lale walks ahead. Baretski catches up.

"What? Did I say something wrong?"

"Do you really want me to answer that?"

"Yeah."

Lale turns to him. "Do you have a sister?"

"Yeah," says Baretski, "two."

"Is how you treat women the way you want other men to treat your sisters?"

"Anyone does that to my kid sister and I'll kill them." Baretski pulls his pistol from its holster and fires several shots into the air. "I'll kill them."

Lale jumps back. The gunshots reverberate around them. Baretski is panting, his face red and his eyes dark.

Lale raises his hands. "Got it. Just something to think about."

"I don't want to talk about this anymore."

⌘

LALE FINDS OUT THAT BARETSKI ISN'T GERMAN BUT WAS BORN in Romania, in a small town near the border of Slovakia, only a few hundred miles from Lale's hometown of Krompachy. He ran away from home to Berlin and joined the Hitler Youth and then the SS. He hates his father, who used to beat him and his brothers and sisters viciously. He is worried about his sisters, one younger, one older, who still live at home.

Later that night as they walk back to Birkenau, Lale says quietly, "I'll take your offer of paper and pencil, if you don't mind. Her number is 34902."

After dinner, Lale slips quietly over to Block 7. The kapo glares at him but says nothing.

Lale shares his extra evening rations, only a few crusts of bread, with his friends from the block. The men talk and exchange news. As usual, the religious among them invite Lale to partake in evening prayer. He politely declines, and his refusal is politely accepted. This is the standard routine.

～

ALONE IN HIS SINGLE ROOM, LALE WAKES TO THE SIGHT OF Baretski standing over him. He didn't knock before entering—he never has—but there is something different about this visit.

"She's in Block 29." He hands Lale a pencil and some paper. "Here, write to her and I will make sure she gets it."

"Do you know her name?"

Baretski's look gives Lale his answer. *What do you think?*

"I'll come back in an hour and take it to her."

"Make it two."

Lale agonizes over the first words he will write to prisoner 34902. *How to even begin? How to address her?* Eventually he decides to keep it simple: "Hello, my name is Lale." When Baretski returns, he hands him the page, only a few sentences on it. He has told her he is from Krompachy in Slovakia, his age, and the makeup of his family, who he hopes are safe. He asks her to be near the administration building next Sunday morning. He explains that he will try to be there, too, and that if he isn't, it will be because of his work, which isn't regulated like everyone else's.

Baretski takes the letter and reads it in front of Lale.

"Is this all you have to say?"

"Anything more, I'll say in person."

Baretski sits down on Lale's bed and leans in to boast about what he would say, what he would do if he was in Lale's situation— that is, not knowing if he will still be alive at the end of the week. Lale thanks him for the input but says he prefers to take his chances.

"Fine. I'll deliver this so-called *letter* to her and give her pencil and paper to reply. I'll tell her I will come for her reply tomorrow morning—give her all night to think about whether or not she likes you."

He smirks at Lale as he leaves the room.

What have I done? He has placed prisoner 34902 in danger. He is protected. She is not. And still, he wants, needs, to take the risk.

❧

THE NEXT DAY, LALE AND LEON WORK WELL INTO THE EVE-ning. Baretski patrols not far from them at all times, often exercising his authority with the lines of men, using his rifle as a baton when he doesn't like the look of someone. His insidious smirk is never off his face. He takes clear delight in swaggering up and down the rows of men. It is only when Lale and Leon are packing up that he takes a piece of paper from his jacket pocket and hands it to Lale.

"Oh, Tätowierer," he says, "she doesn't say much. I think you should choose yourself another girlfriend."

As Lale reaches out to take the note, Baretski playfully pulls it away. *OK, if that's the way you want to play it.* He turns and walks away. Baretski chases after him and gives him the note. A curt nod of the head is the only thanks Lale is prepared to give him. Putting the note in his bag, he walks toward his evening meal, watching Leon head back to his block, knowing he will probably have missed his own.

There is a small amount of food left by the time Lale arrives. After eating, he shoves several pieces of bread up his sleeve, cursing the fact that his Russian uniform has been replaced by a pajama-like outfit with no pockets. On entering Block 7, he receives the usual quiet chorus of greeting. He explains that he only has enough extra food for Leon and maybe two others, promising that he will try to get more tomorrow. He cuts his stay short and hurries back to his room. He needs to read the words buried among his tools.

He drops onto his bed and holds the note to his chest, picturing prisoner 34902 writing the words he is so eager to read. Finally, he opens it.

"Dear Lale," it begins. Like him, the woman has written only a few careful lines. She is also from Slovakia. She has been in Auschwitz longer than Lale, since early April. She works in one of the warehouses nicknamed "Canada," where prisoners sort through the belongings confiscated from fellow victims. She will be in the compound on Sunday and will look for him. Lale rereads the note and turns the paper over several times. Grabbing the pencil from his bag, he scribbles in bold on the back of her letter: *Your name, what is your name?*

⤚⤙

THE NEXT MORNING, BARETSKI ESCORTS LALE TO AUSCHWITZ alone. The new transport is a small one, so Leon has been given a day's rest. Baretski begins to tease Lale about the note and how he must have lost his touch with the ladies. Lale ignores his teasing, asks him if he's read any good books lately.

"Books? I don't read books," Baretski mutters.

"You should."

"Why? What good are books?"

"You can learn a lot from them, and girls like it if you can quote lines or recite poetry."

"I don't need to quote books. I've got this uniform; that's all I need to get girls. They love the uniform. I have a girlfriend, you know," Baretski boasts.

This is news to Lale.

"That's nice. And she likes your uniform?"

"Sure does. She even puts it on and marches around saluting—thinks she's Hitler." With a chilling laugh he mimics her, strutting away, arm raised: "Heil Hitler! Heil Hitler!"

"Just because she likes your uniform doesn't mean she likes you," blurts out Lale.

Baretski stops in his tracks.

Lale curses himself for the careless comment. He slows his steps, pondering whether to go back and apologize. No, he'll walk on and see what happens. Closing his eyes, he places one foot in front of the other, one step at a time, waiting, expecting to hear the shot. He hears the sound of running behind him. Then the tug of an arm on his sleeve. "Is that what you think, Tätowierer? That she just likes me because of my uniform?"

A relieved Lale turns to face him. "How do I know what she likes? Why don't you tell me something else about her?"

He doesn't want any part of this conversation, but having dodged a bullet, he feels he has no choice. It turns out that Baretski knows very little about his "girlfriend," mostly because he's never asked her about herself. This is too much for Lale to ignore, and before he knows it he is giving Baretski further advice on how to treat women. Inside his head, Lale is telling himself to shut up. What should he care about the monster beside him and whether or not he will ever be capable of treating a woman with respect? In truth, he hopes Baretski will not survive this place to be with any woman ever again.

5

Sunday morning has arrived. Lale leaps from his bed and hurries outside. The sun is up. *Where is everybody? Where are the birds? Why aren't they singing?*

"It's Sunday!" he calls to no one in particular. Spinning around, he notices rifles trained on him from the nearby guard towers.

"Oh, shit." He races back into his block as gunshots pierce the quiet dawn. The guard seems to have decided to scare him. Lale knows this is the one day that prisoners "sleep in," or at least don't leave their blocks until their hunger pains force them toward the black coffee and a single piece of stale bread. The guard sends another round into the building, for the fun of it.

Back in his small room, Lale paces to and fro, rehearsing the first words he will say to her.

You're the most beautiful girl I've ever seen is given a run, and discarded. He feels pretty sure that with her bald head and clothes once worn by someone much bigger, she doesn't feel beautiful.

Still, he won't completely rule it out. But perhaps the best thing would be to keep it simple—*What is your name?*—and see where that leads.

Lale forces himself to stay inside until he begins to hear the sounds, so familiar to him now, of the camp waking up. First, the siren pierces the prisoners' sleep. Then hungover SS, short on sleep and temper, bark instructions. The breakfast urns clang as they are moved to each block; the prisoners carrying them groan as they get weaker by the day and the urns get heavier by the minute.

He wanders over to his breakfast station and joins the other men who qualify for extra rations. There is the usual nodding of heads, raising of eyes, occasional brief smiles. No words are exchanged. He eats half his bread, stuffing the remainder up his sleeve, creating a cuff to keep it from falling out. If he can, he will offer it to her. If not, it will be Leon's.

He watches as those not working mingle with friends from other blocks and disperse in small groups to sit and enjoy the summer sun while it lasts. Autumn is just around the corner. He starts toward the compound to begin his search, and then realizes that his bag is missing. *My lifeline.* He never leaves his room without it, yet this morning he has. *Where is my head?* He runs back to his block and reappears, head up, bag in hand—a man on a mission.

❦

FOR WHAT SEEMS LIKE A LONG TIME LALE WALKS AMONG HIS fellow prisoners, chatting to those he knows from Block 7. All the while, his eyes search the groups of girls. He is talking to Leon

THE TATTOOIST OF AUSCHWITZ

when the tiny hairs on the back of his neck rise—the tickling sensation of being watched. He turns. There she is.

She is chatting with three other girls. Noticing that he has seen her, she stops. Lale walks toward the girls, and her friends step back, putting a little distance between them and the stranger; they have heard about Lale. She is left standing alone.

He comes close to the girl, drawn again to her eyes. Her friends giggle quietly in the background. She smiles. A weak, tentative smile. Lale is almost rendered speechless. But he summons the courage. He hands her the bread and letter. In it, unable to stop himself, he has told her that he can't stop thinking about her.

"What's your name?" he asks. "I need to know your name."

Behind him someone says, "Gita."

Before he is able to do or say anything more, Gita's friends rush to her and drag her away, whispering questions as they go.

That night, Lale lies on his bed saying her name over and over. "Gita. Gita. What a beautiful name."

⁓

IN BLOCK 29 IN THE WOMEN'S CAMP, GITA CURLS UP WITH HER friends Dana and Ivana. A beam from a floodlight seeps through a small crack in the timber wall, and Gita strains to read Lale's letter.

"How many times are you going to read it?" Dana asks.

"Oh, I don't know, until I know every word by heart," Gita replies.

"When will that be?"

"About two hours ago," Gita giggles. Dana hugs her friend tightly.

❧

THE NEXT MORNING, GITA AND DANA ARE THE LAST TO LEAVE their block. They exit with their arms linked, talking, oblivious to their surroundings. Without warning, the SS officer outside their block hits Gita in the back with his rifle. Both girls crash to the ground. Gita cries out in pain. He indicates with his rifle for them to get up. They stand, their eyes downcast.

He looks at them with disgust and snarls, "Wipe the smile from your face." He takes his pistol from its holster and pushes it hard against Gita's temple. He gives the instruction to another officer: "No food for them today."

As he walks away, their kapo advances and slaps them both quickly across the face. "Don't forget where you are." She walks away, and Gita rests her head on Dana's shoulder.

"I told you Lale's going to talk to me next Sunday, didn't I?"

❧

SUNDAY. PRISONERS MEANDER AROUND THE COMPOUND, ALONE and in small groups. Some sit up against the buildings, too tired and weak to move. A handful of SS roam about, chatting and smoking, ignoring the prisoners. Gita and her friends walk around, keeping their faces blank. All but Gita talk quietly. She is looking around her.

Lale watches Gita and her friends, smiling at Gita's worried look. Whenever her eyes almost land on him, he ducks behind other prisoners. He moves slowly toward her. Dana sees him first and is about to say something when Lale holds a finger to his lips. Without breaking step, he reaches out, takes Gita by the hand, and continues walking. Her friends giggle and grasp each other as Lale silently steers Gita around the back of the administration building, checking to make sure the guard in the nearby tower is relaxed and not looking in their direction.

He slides his back down the wall of the building, pulling Gita with him. From there, they can see the forest beyond the perimeter fence. Gita peers down at the ground while Lale looks intently at her.

"Hello . . ." he says tentatively.

"Hello," she replies.

"I hope I haven't frightened you."

"Are we safe?" She darts a look at the nearby guard tower.

"Probably not, but I can't go on just seeing you. I need to be with you and talk to you, like people should."

"But we're not safe—"

"It's never going to be safe. Talk to me. I want to hear your voice. I want to know all about you. All I know is your name. Gita. It's beautiful."

"What do you want me to say?"

Lale struggles for the right question. He goes for something ordinary. "How about . . . how's your day been?"

Now she lifts her head and looks him straight in the eye. "Oh, you know how it is. Got up, had a big breakfast, kissed Mama and Papa goodbye before catching the bus to work. Work was—"

"OK, OK, I'm sorry, dumb question."

They sit side by side but look away from each other. Lale listens to Gita's breathing. She taps a thumb against her thigh. Finally, she says, "So how is your day going?"

"Oh, you know. Got up, had a big breakfast . . ."

They look at each other and laugh quietly. Gita gently nudges Lale. Their hands accidentally touch for an instant.

"Well, if we can't talk about our day, tell me something about yourself," Lale says.

"There's nothing to tell."

Lale is taken aback. "Of course there is. What's your last name?"

She stares at Lale, shaking her head. "I'm just a number. You should know that. You gave it to me."

"Yes, but that's just in here. Who are you outside of here?"

"Outside doesn't exist anymore. There's only here."

Lale stands up and stares at her. "My name is Ludwig Eisenberg, but people call me Lale. I come from Krompachy, Slovakia. I have a mother, a father, a brother, and a sister." He pauses. "Now it's your turn."

Gita meets his stare defiantly. "I am prisoner 34902 in Birkenau, Poland."

Conversation fades into uneasy silence. He watches her, her downcast eyes. She is struggling with her thoughts: what to say, what not to say.

Lale sits back down, in front of her this time. He reaches out as if to take her hand, then withdraws it. "I don't want to upset you, but will you promise me one thing?"

"What?"

"That before we leave here, you will tell me who you are and where you come from."

She looks him in the eye. "Yes, I promise."

"I'm happy with that for now. So, they've got you working in the Canada?"

Gita nods.

"Is it OK there?"

"It's OK. But the Germans just throw all the prisoners' possessions in together. Rotten food mixed with clothing. And the mold—I hate touching it, and it stinks."

"I'm glad you're not outside. I've spoken to some men who know girls from their villages who also work in the Canada. They tell me they often find jewels and money."

"I've heard that. I just seem to find moldy bread."

"You will be careful, won't you? Don't do anything silly, and always keep your eye on the SS."

"I've learned that lesson well, trust me."

A siren sounds.

"You'd better get back to your block," says Lale. "Next time I'll bring some food for you."

"You have food?"

"I can get extra. I'll get it to you, and I'll see you next Sunday."

Lale stands and holds his hand out to Gita. She takes it. He pulls her to her feet, holds her hand a moment longer than he should. He can't take his eyes off her.

"We should go." She breaks eye contact, but maintains her spell over him with a smile that makes his knees go weak.

6

Weeks have gone by; the trees surrounding the camp have dropped their leaves, the days have become shorter as winter advances.

Who are those people? Lale has been asking himself this question ever since he arrived in the camp. The groups of men who work on the construction sites who appear every day dressed in civilian clothing, never to be seen after "tools down." With a spring in his step from his time with Gita, Lale feels sure he can talk to a couple of the men without the SS getting worked up and taking a shot at him. And he has his bag-shaped shield.

Lale strolls casually toward one of the new brick buildings under construction. These don't seem to be blocks to house prisoners, but their use is of no concern to Lale today. He approaches two men, one older than the other, busily engaged in bricklaying, and squats down beside a pile of bricks awaiting placement. The two men watch him with interest, slowing their work rate. Lale picks up a brick and pretends to study it.

"I don't get it," he says quietly.

"What don't you get?" the older man asks.

"I'm a Jew. They've branded me with a yellow star. Around me I see political prisoners, murderers, and lazy men who won't work. And then you—you wear no brand."

"That's none of your business, Jew boy," says the younger man, himself no more than a boy.

"Just being friendly. You know how it is—I was checking out my surroundings and became curious about you and your friends. My name is Lale."

"Get lost!" the young one says.

"Settle down, boy. Don't mind him," the older man says to Lale, his voice rough from too many cigarettes. "My name's Victor. The mouth here is my son, Yuri." Victor extends his hand, which Lale shakes. Lale then offers his hand to Yuri, but he doesn't take it.

"We live nearby," Victor explains, "so we come here to work each day."

"I just want to get this straight. You come here each day voluntarily? I mean, you're paid to be here?"

Yuri pipes up. "That's right, Jew boy, we get paid and go home every night. But you—"

"I said shut up, Yuri. Can't you see the man's just being friendly?"

"Thanks, Victor. I'm not here to cause trouble. Like I said, just checking things out."

"What's the bag for?" snaps Yuri, smarting at having been reprimanded in front of Lale.

"My tools. My tools for tattooing the numbers on the prisoners. I'm the Tätowierer."

"Busy job," quips Victor.

"Some days. I never know when transports are coming, or how big they'll be."

"I hear there's worse to come."

"Are you prepared to tell me?"

"This building. I've seen the plans. You're not going to like what it is."

"Surely it can't be any worse than what's going on here already." Lale is now standing, bracing himself on the pile of bricks.

"It's called Crematorium One," Victor says quietly, and looks away.

"Crematorium. One. With the possibility of a number two?"

"Sorry. I said you wouldn't like it."

Lale punches the last brick laid, sending it flying, and shakes his hand in pain.

Victor reaches into a nearby bag and produces a piece of dried sausage wrapped in waxed paper.

"Here, take this. I know they're starving you people, and I've got plenty where this came from."

"That's our lunch!" Yuri cries, rushing to take the sausage from his father's outstretched hand.

Victor pushes Yuri away. "It won't hurt you to go without for a day. This man needs it more."

"I'm gonna tell Mum when we get home."

"You'd better hope I don't tell her about your attitude. You've got a lot to learn about being civilized, young man. Let this be your first lesson."

Lale still hasn't taken the sausage. "I'm sorry. I didn't mean to cause trouble."

"Well, you have," wails a petulant Yuri.

"No, he hasn't," says Victor. "Lale, take the sausage, and come and see us again tomorrow. I'll have more for you. Hell, if we can help just one of you, we'll do it. Right, Yuri?"

Yuri reluctantly extends his hand to Lale, who takes it.

"Save the one, save the world," Lale says quietly, more to himself than the others.

"I can't help you all."

Lale takes the food. "I don't have anything to pay you with."

"It's not a problem."

"Thank you. There might be a way I could pay you, though. If I find a way, can you get me something else, like chocolate?" He wanted chocolate. That's what you give a girl if you can get it.

"I'm sure we can work something out. You'd better move on; there's an officer paying us some attention."

"See you," Lale says as he shoves the sausage into his bag. Stray snowflakes drift around him as he walks back to his block. The flakes catch in the last rays of the sun, bouncing strobes of light that remind him of a kaleidoscope he played with as a boy. *What's wrong with this picture?* Lale is overcome with emotion as he hurries back to his block. On his face, the melted snow is indistinguishable from the tears. The winter of 1942 has arrived.

⤳

BACK IN HIS ROOM, LALE TAKES THE CHUNK OF SAUSAGE AND breaks it carefully into even parts. He tears strips from the waxed paper and wraps each piece tightly before placing them back in his bag. As he comes to the last piece, Lale stops and considers the small, fulfilling parcel of food, sitting there next to his rough, dirty fingers. The fingers that used to be smooth and clean and plump, that handled rich food, that he used to hold up to tell hosts, "No, thank you, I couldn't possibly have any more." With a shake of his head, he places it, too, into the bag.

He heads toward one of the Canada buildings. He once asked a man in Block 7 if he knew why they called the sorting rooms by that name.

"The girls who work there dream of a place far away where there is plenty of everything and life can be what they want it to be. They have decided Canada is such a place."

Lale has spoken to a couple of the girls working in this one as they returned to their block in the afternoon. He has checked everyone exiting many times and knows that Gita doesn't work at this one. There are other buildings he cannot easily access; she must work in one of them. He spies two girls he has spoken to before, walking together. He reaches into his bag, withdraws two parcels, and approaches them, smiling. He turns and walks alongside them.

"I want you to put out one of your hands, but do it slowly. I'm going to give you a parcel of sausage. Do not open it until you're alone."

The two girls do as he says, not breaking step, their eyes darting about for SS who might be watching them. Once the sausage is in their hands, they wrap their arms across their chests, as much to keep themselves warm as to protect their gift.

"Girls, I've heard you sometimes find jewels and money—is that correct?"

The women exchange a glance.

"Now, I don't want to put you at risk, but do you think there's any way you could smuggle a little of it out to me?"

One of them says nervously, "Shouldn't be too hard. Our minders don't pay much attention to us anymore. They think we're harmless."

"Great. Just get what you can without causing suspicion, and I'll use it to buy you and others food, like this sausage."

"Do you think you could get some chocolate?" one of them says, her eyes bright.

"Can't promise, but I'll try. Remember, only take small quantities at a time. I'll try to be here tomorrow afternoon. If I'm not, is there somewhere safe you can hide things until I can get to you?"

"Not in our block. We can't do that. We get searched all the time," one replies.

"I know," says the other. "The snow is piling up at the back of our block. We can wrap them in a rag and hide it there when we go to the toilet."

"Yeah, that will work," the first one says.

"You can't tell anyone what you're doing or where you're getting the food from, OK? It's really important. Your lives depend upon you saying nothing. Got that?"

One of the girls draws her finger across her closed mouth. As they near the women's compound, Lale splits off from them and loiters outside Block 29 for a short time. There is no sign of Gita. So it must be. But it will be Sunday again in three days' time.

❧

THE NEXT DAY, LALE COMPLETES HIS WORK AT BIRKENAU within a few hours. Leon asks him to spend the afternoon with him, wanting the opportunity to talk about their situation without a block full of men straining to hear every word. Lale begs off, saying he isn't feeling well and needs to get some rest. They go their separate ways.

He is conflicted. He desperately wants whatever food Victor has brought, but he needs something to pay him with. The girls finish work around the same time that Victor and the other visiting workers leave. Will he have enough time to see if they have managed to lift anything? In the end he decides to visit Victor and reassure him that he is working on obtaining a source of payment.

Bag in hand, Lale makes his way over to the block under construction. He looks around for Victor and Yuri. Victor sees him and nudges Yuri to follow as they separate from the other workers. Slowly they approach Lale, who has stopped and is pretending to be looking for something in his bag. With an outstretched hand, Yuri greets Lale.

"His mother had a word with him last night," offers Victor.

"I'm sorry, I haven't been able to get anything to pay you with, but I hope to have something very soon. Please don't bring anything else until I've paid you for what you've given me already."

"It's OK, we have plenty to spare," Victor says.

"No, you're taking a risk. At the very least, you should get something in return. Just give me a day or two."

Victor takes from his bag two packages, which he drops into Lale's open bag. "We'll be here at the same time tomorrow."

"Thank you," says Lale.

"See you," says Yuri, which makes Lale smile.

"See you, Yuri."

꧁꧂

BACK IN HIS ROOM, LALE OPENS THE PACKAGES. SAUSAGE AND chocolate. He holds the chocolate to his nose and inhales.

Once again, he breaks the food into small pieces to make it easy for the girls to hide and pass around. Oh, how he hopes they will be discreet. The consequences if they aren't don't bear thinking about. He saves a small amount of the sausage for Block 7. The tools-down siren interrupts his obsessive efforts to ensure that each piece of food is exactly the same size. He throws everything into his bag and hurries toward the Canada.

Not far from the women's compound, Lale catches up with his two friends. They see him coming and slow their pace, dropping back into the mob of girls trudging "home." He holds the food bundles in one hand, the open bag in the other, and nudges the girls. Without looking at him, each girl drops something into his bag, and he in turn presses the food into their hands. They shove it up their sleeves. Lale and the girls split away from each other at the entrance to the women's compound.

Lale doesn't know what he will find in the four pieces of rag that he places on his bed. He opens them gently. They contain coins and Polish zloty bills, loose diamonds, rubies and sapphires, gold and silver rings emblazoned with precious stones. Lale steps back, knocking into the door behind him. He is recoiling from the sad provenance of these objects, each one attached to a momentous event in the life of its previous owner. He is also scared for his own safety. If he is discovered with this bounty, he will surely be put to death. A noise outside makes him throw the jewels and currency back in his bag, and himself on his bed. No one comes in. Eventually he rises and takes his bag with him to his evening meal. In the canteen he doesn't place his bag at his feet as usual, but clings to it with one hand, trying not to look too strange. He suspects he fails.

Later that night he separates the precious stones from the money, the loose gems from the jewelry, wrapping them separately in the rags they came in. The majority of the loot he pushes under his mattress. He keeps a loose ruby and a diamond ring in his bag.

AT SEVEN THE NEXT MORNING, LALE HANGS AROUND THE main compound gates as the local workers enter. He sidles up to Victor and opens his hand to reveal the ruby and the ring. Victor closes his hand over Lale's in a handshake, palming the jewels. Lale's bag is already open, and Victor quickly transfers some packages into it. Their alliance is now sealed.

Victor whispers, "Happy New Year."

Lale trudges away, the snow now falling heavily and covering the camp. 1943 has begun.

7

THOUGH IT IS BITTERLY COLD AND THE COMPOUND IS A MESS of snow and mud, Lale is upbeat. It is a Sunday. Lale and Gita will be among the brave souls walking in the compound, in the hope of a fleeting meeting, a word, a touch of the hand.

He is pacing, on the lookout for Gita as he attempts to keep the cold out of his bones. He walks by the women's camp as often as he can without raising suspicion. Several girls come from Block 29, but no Gita. Just as he is about to give up, Dana appears, scanning the compound. Spotting Lale, she hurries over.

"Gita's sick," she says as soon as she's in earshot. "She's sick, Lale. I don't know what to do."

His heart lurches to his throat in panic as he remembers the death cart, the close call, the men who nursed him back to health. "I have to see her."

"You can't go in—our kapo is in a terrible mood. She wants to call the SS and have them take Gita away."

"You can't let them. You mustn't let them take her. Please, Dana," says Lale. "What's wrong with her? Do you know?"

"We think it's typhus. We've lost several girls in our block this week."

"Then she needs medicine, penicillin."

"And where are we gonna get medicine, Lale? If we go to the hospital and ask for penicillin, they'll just take her away. I can't lose her. I've lost all my family. Please, can you help us, Lale?" Dana pleads.

"Don't take her to the hospital. Whatever you do, don't go there." Lale's mind races. "Listen to me, Dana—it's going to take me a couple of days, but I'm going to try to get her some penicillin." A numbness sweeps over him. His vision blurs. His head pounds.

"Here's what you have to do. Tomorrow morning take her, however you can—carry, drag, whatever—take her to the Canada. Hide her there among the clothes in the day, try to get as much water into her as you can, then bring her back to your block for roll call. You might have to do this for a few days until I can get medicine, but you must do it. It's the only way to stop her from being taken to the hospital. Now go and look after her."

"All right, I can do that. Ivana will help. But she must have medicine."

He grips Dana's hand. "Tell her . . ."

Dana waits.

"Tell her I will take care of her."

Lale watches Dana run back into her block. He can't move. Thoughts creep into his head. He sees the death cart every day— Black Mary, it's called. She cannot end up there. That must not be her fate. He looks around at the brave souls who have ventured outside. He imagines them dropping into the snow and lying there, smiling up at him, thankful that death has taken them from this place.

"You cannot have her. I will not let you take her from me," he calls.

Prisoners move away from him. The SS have chosen to stay inside on this bleak, dark day and soon Lale finds himself alone, paralyzed by cold and fear. Finally he begins to move his feet. His mind rejoins the rest of his body. And he stumbles back to his room and collapses on his bed.

DAYLIGHT CREEPS INTO HIS ROOM THE NEXT MORNING. THE room feels empty, even of him. Looking down from above, he does not see himself. An out-of-body experience. *Where have I gone? I have to come back. There's something important for me to do.* The memory of yesterday's meeting with Dana jolts him back to reality.

He grabs his bag and his boots, throws a blanket around his shoulders, and runs from his room to the front gates. He doesn't check who is around. He must get to Victor and Yuri immediately.

The two men arrive with the others in their detail, sinking into the snow with each step they take toward work. They see Lale and move away from the others, meeting him halfway. He shows Victor the gems and currency in his hand, a small fortune's worth. Everything he has, he drops into Victor's bag.

"Penicillin or something similar," Lale says. "Can you help me?"

Victor places his packages of food into Lale's open bag and nods. "Yes."

Lale hurries over to Block 29 and watches from a distance. *Where are they? Why haven't they appeared?* He paces up and down, oblivious to the eyes in the towers surrounding the camp.

He must see Gita. She has to have made it through the night. Finally he sees Dana and Ivana, with Gita hanging weakly from their shoulders. Two other girls help to block the scene from easy view. Lale drops to his knees at the thought that this could be the last time he sees her.

"What are you doing down there?" Baretski appears behind him.

He staggers to his feet. "I was feeling sick, but I'm OK now."

"Maybe you should see a doctor. You know we have several at Auschwitz."

"No, thanks, I'd rather ask you to shoot me."

Baretski withdraws his pistol from its holster. "If this is where you want to die, Tätowierer, I would be happy to oblige."

"I'm sure you would, but not today," Lale says. "I take it we've got work to do?"

Baretski holsters his gun. "Auschwitz," he says as he begins walking. "And take that blanket back to where you found it. You look ridiculous."

⁓

LALE AND LEON SPEND THE MORNING AT AUSCHWITZ, tattooing numbers on frightened newcomers and attempting to soften the shock of it. But Lale's mind is on Gita, and several times he presses too hard.

In the afternoon, when the job is finished, Lale half walks, half runs back to Birkenau. He meets Dana near the entrance to Block 29 and gives her all his rations from breakfast.

"We made a bed for her out of clothing," Dana says as she folds the food into makeshift shirt cuffs, "and we gave her pieces of snow for water. We took her back to the block this afternoon, but she's still in a really bad way."

Lale squeezes Dana's hand. "Thank you. Try to get some food into her. I'll have medicine tomorrow."

He departs, his mind a whirlpool. *I barely know Gita, yet how can I live if she does not?*

That night, sleep evades him.

The next morning, Victor places medicine, along with food, into Lale's bag.

That afternoon, he is able to get it to Dana.

⁓

IN THE EVENING, DANA AND IVANA SIT BESIDE A NOW FULLY unconscious Gita. The pull of typhus is stronger than they are; the black stillness has completely overtaken her. They talk to her, but she gives no sign that she hears them. From a small vial, Dana places several drops of liquid into Gita's mouth as Ivana holds it open.

"I don't think I can keep carrying her to the Canada," an exhausted Ivana says.

"She will get better," Dana insists. "Just a few more days."

"Where did Lale get the medicine from?"

"We don't need to know. Just be grateful that he did."

"Do you think it's too late?"

"I don't know, Ivana. Let's just hold her tight and get her through the night."

⁓

THE NEXT MORNING, LALE WATCHES FROM A DISTANCE AS GITA is once again carried toward the Canada. He sees her attempt to raise her head on a couple of occasions and is overjoyed at the sight. He now needs to seek out Baretski.

The main SS officers' quarters are at Auschwitz. There is just a small building for them at Birkenau, and it is there that Lale goes in the hope of catching Baretski as he is coming or going. He appears after several hours and seems surprised to see Lale waiting for him.

"Not enough work for you, eh?" Baretski asks.

"I have a favor to ask," Lale blurts out.

Baretski narrows his eyes. "I won't do any more favors."

"Maybe one day I can do something for you."

Baretski laughs. "What could you possibly do for me?"

"You never know, but wouldn't you like to bank a favor, just in case?"

Baretski sighs. "What do you want?"

"It's Gita . . ."

"Your girlfriend."

"Can you get her transferred from the Canada into the administration building?"

"Why? I suppose you want her where there's heating?"

"Yes."

Baretski taps a foot. "It might take me a day or two, but I'll see what I can do. No promises."

"Thank you."

"You owe me, Tätowierer." The smirk is back as he fondles his swagger stick. "You owe me."

With more bravado than he feels, Lale says, "Not yet I don't, but I hope to." He walks away, a small spring in his step. Perhaps he can make Gita's life a little more bearable.

❧

THE FOLLOWING SUNDAY, LALE WALKS SLOWLY ALONGSIDE A recovering Gita. He wants to put his arm around her like he saw

Dana and Ivana do, but he doesn't dare. It is good enough to be near her. It doesn't take long for her to be exhausted, and it is too cold to sit. She wears a long woolen coat, no doubt something the girls have appropriated from the Canada with no objection from the SS. It has deep pockets and Lale fills them with food before he sends her back to her block to rest.

⁓

THE FOLLOWING MORNING, A TREMBLING GITA IS ESCORTED into the main administration building by an SS officer. The young woman has been told nothing and she automatically fears the worst. She has been sick, and now she is weak—clearly the authorities have decided she is no longer of use. As the officer speaks to a more senior colleague, Gita looks around the large room. It is filled with drab green desks and filing cabinets. Nothing is out of place. What strikes her most is the warmth. The SS work here, too, so of course there is heating. A mixture of female prisoners and female civilians work quickly and quietly, writing, filing, heads down.

The escorting officer directs Gita toward her colleague, and Gita stumbles, still suffering the aftereffects of the typhus. The colleague breaks her fall before roughly shoving her away. She then grabs Gita's arm and inspects her tattoo before dragging her toward an empty desk and shoving her down on a hard wooden chair, next to another prisoner dressed just like her. The girl doesn't look up, only tries to make herself smaller, unobtrusive, so the officer will ignore her.

"Put her to work," the grumpy officer barks.

Once they're alone, the girl shows Gita a long list of names and details. She hands her a pile of cards and indicates that she is to transcribe the details of each person first onto a card and then into the large leather-bound book between them. No words are spoken, and a quick glance around the room tells Gita to keep her mouth shut, too.

Later that day, Gita hears a familiar voice and looks up. Lale has entered the room and is handing papers to one of the civilian girls working at the front desk. Finishing his conversation, he slowly scans all the faces. As his glance passes Gita, he winks. She can't help herself—she gasps, and a few women turn to look at her. The girl beside her nudges her in the ribs as Lale hurries from the room.

❧

WITH THE DAY'S WORK ENDED, GITA SEES LALE STANDING A distance away, watching the girls leave the administration building for their blocks. The heavy SS presence prevents him from approaching. As the girls walk together, they talk.

"I'm Cilka," Gita's new colleague says. "I'm in Block 25."

"I'm Gita, Block 29."

As the girls enter the women's camp, Dana and Ivana rush to Gita.

"Are you all right? Where did they take you? *Why* did they take you?" Dana demands, fear and relief on her face.

"I'm OK. They took me to work in the administration office."

"How . . . ?" Ivana asks.

"Lale. I think he somehow arranged it."

"But you're all right. They didn't hurt you?"

"I'm fine. This is Cilka. I'm working with her."

Dana and Ivana greet Cilka with a hug. Gita smiles, happy that her friends are so immediately accepting of another girl in their midst. All afternoon she had worried how they would re-act to her now working in relative comfort, without having to deal with the cold or any physical effort. She could hardly blame them if they were jealous of her new role and felt she was no longer one of them.

"I'd better go to my block," says Cilka. "I'll see you tomorrow, Gita."

Cilka walks off, and Ivana watches her go. "Gosh, she's pretty. Even dressed in rags, she's beautiful."

"Yes, she is. She's been throwing me little smiles all day, just enough to reassure me. Her beauty goes beyond the surface."

Cilka turns back and smiles at the three of them. Then, with one hand, she removes the scarf from her head and waves it to them, revealing long dark hair cascading down her back. She moves with the grace of a swan, a young woman unaware of her own beauty and seemingly untouched by the horror around her.

"You must ask her how she has kept her hair," Ivana says, scratching absently at her own headscarf.

Gita pulls her own scarf from her head and runs her hand over her short, spiky stubble, knowing all too well that it will soon be removed again, shaved back to her scalp. Her smile disappears briefly. Then she replaces her scarf and links arms with Dana and Ivana, and they walk toward the meal cart.

8

LALE AND LEON HAVE BEEN WORKING AROUND THE CLOCK AS the Germans storm every city, town, and village and empty them of Jews; those from France, Belgium, Yugoslavia, Italy, Moravia, Greece, and Norway join prisoners already taken from Czechoslovakia, Germany, Austria, Poland, and Slovakia. At Auschwitz, they tattoo those unfortunate enough to be selected by the "medical team." Those designated to work are brought in trains to Birkenau, which saves Lale and Leon a round-trip walk of five miles. But with this many new arrivals, Lale doesn't have time to collect the loot from the girls in the Canada, and Victor's treats go back home with him each day. Once in a while, when the numbers have dwindled and the time of day is right, Lale begs off for a toilet break and makes it to the Canada. The hoard of gems, jewelry, and currency under his mattress increases.

Day has become night and still men line up to be numbered for life, be it short or long. Lale works robotically, reaching for the paper, taking the offered arm, numbering. "Move on." "Next, please." He knew he was tired, but the next arm is so heavy that he drops it. A giant of a man stands before him, all chest and thick neck and massive limbs.

"I'm very hungry," whispers the man.

Lale then does something he has never done before. "What's your name?" he asks.

"Jakub."

Lale sets about tattooing Jakub's number. When he has finished, he looks around and observes that the SS guarding them are tired and paying little attention to what is going on. Lale ushers Jakub behind him, into the shadows where the floodlights do not reach.

"Wait there until I'm finished."

When the last prisoner has been numbered, Lale and Leon gather up their tools and tables. Lale waves goodbye to Leon and apologizes that he has again missed his evening meal, promising to bring him something from his stash tomorrow morning. *Or is it this morning?* With Jakub still hidden, Lale stalls, making sure all the SS have moved on. Finally, there is no one around. A quick glance at the tower posts reveals no one looking their way. He instructs Jakub to follow him, and they hurry to Lale's room. Lale closes the door behind them and Jakub sits down on Lale's bed. Lale lifts one corner of the sunken mattress to produce some bread and sausage. He offers it to the man, and Jakub makes short work of it.

When he has finished eating, Lale asks, "Where are you from?"

"America."

"How did you end up *here?*"

"I was visiting my family in Poland and got trapped here—I

couldn't leave—and then we got rounded up, and here I am. I don't know where my family is. We got separated."

"But you live in America?"

"Yes."

"Shit, that's tough."

"What's your name?" Jakub asks.

"I'm Lale. They call me the Tätowierer, and, like me, you will do well here."

"I don't understand. What do you mean?"

"Your size. The Germans are the cruelest bastards ever to live, but they are not entirely stupid. They have a knack for finding the right person for the right job, and I'm sure they will find work for you."

"What kind of work?"

"I don't know. You'll have to wait and see. Do you know what block you are assigned to?"

"Block 7."

"Ah, I know it well. Come on, let's sneak you in. You'd better be there to answer when your number is called out in a couple of hours."

⌇

TWO DAYS LATER, IT IS SUNDAY. HAVING WORKED THE PAST five Sundays, Lale has missed Gita terribly. Today the sun is shining down on him as he walks the compound, looking for her. As he rounds the corner of one block, he is startled by cheering and applause. Such noises are unheard of in the camp. Lale pushes his way through a crowd to reach its focus. There, center stage, surrounded by both prisoners and SS, Jakub is performing.

Three men carry a large piece of timber to him. He takes it and tosses it away. Prisoners have to scramble to get out of the way. Another prisoner produces a large metal rod, which Jakub sets about bending in half. The show goes on for some time as heavier and heavier items are brought to Jakub for him to display his strength.

A hush falls over the crowd. Houstek is approaching, guarded by SS. Jakub continues his performance, unaware of his new audience. Houstek watches him raise a piece of steel above his head and twist it. He's seen enough. He gives a nod to the nearby SS, who advance on Jakub. They make no attempt to touch him but point their rifles in the direction they expect him to go.

As the crowd thins, Lale sees Gita. He rushes toward her and her friends. One or two giggle when they see him. The sound is so out of place in this camp of death, and Lale delights in it. Gita beams. Taking her by the arm, he steers her to their spot behind the administration building. The ground is still too cold to sit on, so Gita leans against the building, tilts her face to the sun.

"Close your eyes," Lale says.

"Why?"

"Just do as you're told. Trust me."

Gita closes her eyes.

"Open your mouth."

She opens her eyes.

"Close your eyes and open your mouth."

Gita does so. From his bag, Lale produces a small piece of chocolate. He places it on her lips, letting her feel the texture of it, before slowly pushing it a little farther into her mouth. She presses her tongue against it. Lale pulls it back to her lips. Now moistened, he rubs the chocolate gently across her lips, and she licks it off with delight. When he pushes it into her mouth she bites down, taking a chunk off, opening her eyes wide. Savoring the taste, she says, "Why does chocolate taste so much better when it's fed to you?"

"I don't know. No one has ever fed it to me."

Gita takes the small amount of chocolate Lale still holds in his hand.

"Close your eyes and open your mouth."

The same teasing takes place. After Gita has smeared the last bit of chocolate on Lale's lips, she gently kisses him, licking the chocolate away. He opens his eyes to find hers shut. He pulls her into his arms and they kiss passionately. When Gita finally opens her eyes, she wipes the tears that are running down Lale's face.

"What else have you got in that bag of yours?" she asks playfully.

Lale sniffs, and laughs. "A diamond ring. Or would you prefer an emerald?"

"Oh, I'll have the diamond, thank you," she says, playing along.

Lale rummages around in his bag and produces an exquisite silver ring with a single diamond set in it. Handing it to her, he says, "It's yours."

Gita can't take her eyes off the ring, the sun bouncing off the stone. "Where did you get this?"

"Girls working in one of the Canada buildings find jewels and money for me. That's what I use to buy the food and medicine I've been giving you and the others. Here, take it."

Gita puts her hand out as though to try on the ring, but then pulls back. "No, you keep it. Put it to good use."

"OK." Lale goes to put it back in his bag.

"Stop. Let me look at it one more time."

He holds it between two fingers, turning it this way and that.

"It's the most beautiful thing I've ever seen. Now put it away."

"It's the second most beautiful thing I've ever seen," says Lale, looking at Gita. She blushes and turns her face away.

"I'll have some more of that chocolate, if you have any left."

Lale hands her a small block. She snaps off a piece and places it in her mouth, closing her eyes for a moment. She wraps the rest within her sleeve and tucks it up.

"Come on," he says. "Let's get you back to the girls so you can share it."

Gita reaches up to his face, caresses his cheek. "Thank you."

Lale sways, unbalanced by her proximity.

Gita takes his hand and begins to walk, leading Lale. As they enter the main compound, Lale sees Baretski. He and Gita release hands. He exchanges a glance with her that tells her all she needs to know. He aches at parting from her without a word, and with no certainty about when they will next meet. He walks toward Baretski, who is glaring at him.

"I've been looking for you," says Baretski. "We've got work to do at Auschwitz."

~

ALONG THE ROAD TO AUSCHWITZ, LALE AND BARETSKI pass work details of a few men each, being punished with this Sunday work. Several SS guarding them call out a greeting to Baretski, who ignores them. Something is very wrong with him today. Normally he's quite the talker, but today his whole body seems tense. Ahead, Lale sees three prisoners sitting on the ground, back to back, supporting each other, clearly exhausted. The prisoners look up at Lale and Baretski but make no attempt to move. Without breaking step, Baretski pulls his rifle from his back and fires at them repeatedly.

Lale freezes, his eyes locked on the dead men. Finally, looking back up at the retreating Baretski, Lale recalls the first time he saw such an unprovoked attack on defenseless men—they were sitting on a board in the dark. The first night he arrived at Birkenau flashes before him. Baretski is getting farther away from him and Lale fears he will take his anger out on him next. He hurries to catch up to him but remains a slight distance away. He knows that Baretski knows he is there. Once more, they arrive at the gates into Auschwitz, and Lale looks up at the words emblazoned above: ARBEIT MACHT FREI. He silently curses whatever god may be listening.

9

MARCH 1943

LALE REPORTS TO THE ADMINISTRATION OFFICE TO GET HIS instructions. The weather is improving slowly. There has been no snow for a week. On entering, he sweeps his eyes around the office to make sure Gita is where she should be. There she is, still seated beside Cilka. The two have become very close, and Dana and Ivana seem to have welcomed Cilka fully into their little circle. His customary wink to the two of them is acknowledged with suppressed smiles. He approaches the Polish girl behind the counter.

"Good morning, Bella. It's a lovely day outside."

"Good morning, Lale," Bella responds. "I have your work here. I've been told to tell you that all the numbers today are to have the letter Z in front of them."

Lale looks down at the list of numbers, and sure enough, each one is prefixed with the letter Z.

"Do you know what this signifies?"

"No, Lale, I'm not told anything. You know more than I do. I just follow instructions."

"As do I, Bella. Thanks, I'll see you later."

Holding the instructions, Lale heads out the door.

"Lale," Bella calls out.

He turns back to her. With her head turned toward Gita, she asks, "Haven't you forgotten something?"

Smiling at her, he turns to Gita and raises his eyebrows at her. Several girls hold a hand over their mouth, eyes on the lookout for the SS who oversee their work.

⁓

LEON IS WAITING FOR LALE OUTSIDE. LALE FILLS HIM IN AS they walk to their workstation. Trucks are unloading their cargo nearby, and the men do a double take as they register that there are children among those being helped down, along with older men and women. They have never before seen children at Birkenau.

"Surely we're not marking kids. I won't do that," Leon pronounces.

"Here comes Baretski. He'll tell us what to do. Don't say a word."

Baretski strides up. "I see you've noticed that something's different today, Tätowierer. These are your new companions. You're going to be sharing from now on, so you better be nice to them. They'll outnumber you by quite a lot—a hell of a lot, actually."

Lale says nothing.

"They're the filth of Europe, even worse than you. They're Gypsies, and for reasons I'll never know, the Führer has decided they are to live here, with you. What do you say about that, Tätow-ierer?"

"Are we to number the children?"

"You'll number anyone who hands you a number. I'll leave you to your work. I'm going to be busy at the selection, so don't make me come over here."

As Baretski marches off, Leon stammers, "I won't."

"Let's just wait and see what comes our way."

It doesn't take long for men and women, from babes in arms to hunched-over elderly, to begin making their way to Lale and Leon. They are grateful to learn that the children are not to be numbered, though some who present numbers seem too young to Lale. He does his job, offering smiles to children standing by as he numbers their parents and telling the occasional mother holding an infant what a lovely baby she has. Baretski is well out of earshot. He struggles most in numbering the elderly women, who seem to be the walking dead: vacant eyes, perhaps aware of their imminent fate. To them he offers a "Sorry." He knows they probably don't understand.

⁓

IN THE ADMINISTRATION BUILDING, GITA AND CILKA ARE working at their desks. Two SS officers approach them with no warning. Cilka gasps as one of them grabs her by the arm, jerking her to her feet. Gita watches as Cilka is marched from the room, looking back with confused and pleading eyes. Gita doesn't see the administrative SS officer approach until she is struck across the head by a hand, a clear message to get back to work.

Cilka tries to resist as she is dragged down a long corridor to an unknown part of the building. She is no match for the two men, who, on stopping at a closed door, open it and literally throw her inside. Cilka picks herself up and looks around. A large four-poster bed dominates the room. There is also a dresser, and a bed-side table with a lamp and a chair. Someone sits in the chair. Cilka recognizes him: Schwarzhuber, the head of Birkenau. He is an imposing man, rarely seen in the camp. He sits tapping his tall leather boot with his swagger stick. From an expressionless face, he stares at a space above Cilka's head. Cilka backs up against the door. Her hand goes to the door handle. In a flash, the swagger stick hurtles through the air and strikes Cilka's hand. She cries out in pain and slides down to the floor.

Schwarzhuber walks over to her and picks up his stick. He stands over her. His nostrils distend. He breathes heavily and glares at her. He takes off his hat and throws it across the room. With his other hand, he continues to hit his leg firmly with his swagger stick. With every whack Cilka flinches, expecting to be struck. He uses the stick to push up her shirt. Realizing what is expected, with shaking hands Cilka undoes the top two buttons of her shirt. Schwarzhuber then places his stick under her chin and forces her to rise to her feet. She is dwarfed by the man. His eyes seem to see nothing; this is a man whose soul has died and whose body is waiting to catch up with it.

He holds out both his arms, and she interprets this gesture as "undress me." She takes a step closer, still at arm's length, and begins undoing the many buttons on his jacket. A whack across her back with the stick hurries her up. Schwarzhuber is forced to drop the stick so she can slide his jacket off. Taking it from her, he throws it after his hat. He removes his own shirt. Cilka begins undoing his belt and zipper. Kneeling down, she pulls his trousers down to his ankles but can't get them over his boots.

Off balance, Cilka falls heavily when he pushes her over. Dropping onto his knees, he straddles her. Terrified, Cilka attempts to cover herself as he rips her shirt open. She feels the back of his hand across her face as she closes her eyes and gives in to the inevitable.

~

THAT EVENING, GITA RUNS FROM THE OFFICE TO HER BLOCK, tears streaming down her face. Dana and Ivana find her sobbing on their bunk when they arrive a short time later. She is inconsolable and can only tell them that Cilka has been taken away.

~

IT WAS ONLY GOING TO BE A MATTER OF TIME. SINCE BECOMING the Tätowierer, Lale has had an entire block to himself. Each day upon returning there, he has observed the progress made on the buildings going up around him. Three crematoria now play their part in the planned extinction of an entire people. He is in a clearly defined camp, sleeping in the single room usually reserved in each block for the kapo, even though he is kapo to no one. He has always assumed that sooner or later the empty bunk beds behind him would be filled.

Today, Lale returns to his block and watches the children running around outside playing tag. Life is never going to be the same. Several of the older children run up to him and ask questions he fails to understand. They discover that they can communicate in a bastardized form of Hungarian, albeit not always accurately. He shows his room to those now sharing his block, telling them in his sternest voice that they are never, ever to enter. He knows they understand this, but will they respect it? Only time will tell. He considers his limited understanding of Gypsy culture and wonders if he needs to make alternative storage arrangements for what is under his mattress.

He walks into the block, shakes hands with many of the men, and acknowledges the women, the older women in particular. They know what he does here, and he tries to explain it further. They want to know what is going to happen to them. A reasonable question to which he has no answer. He promises he will tell them anything he hears that might affect them. They seem grateful. Many tell him they have never spoken to a Jew before. He doesn't think he's ever spoken to a Gypsy, either.

That night he has trouble sleeping as he adjusts to the sounds of babies crying and children begging their parents for food.

10

WITHIN DAYS, LALE HAS BEEN MADE AN HONORARY ROMANY. He has learned that the word *Gypsy* is often used derogatorily by non-Romany people. Every time he returns to what is now officially known as the "Gypsy camp," he is greeted by young boys and girls who encircle him and ask him to play, or to dig food from his bag. They know he has access to it—he has shared some with them—but he explains that he will give what he can to the adults to portion out to those in greatest need. Many of the adult men approach him daily, asking if he has any news of their fate. He assures them he will pass on anything he hears. He suggests they accept their situation as best they can and recommends arranging some sort of schooling for the children, even if it is merely telling them stories about their home, their family, their culture.

Lale is happy to see them pursue this suggestion, and delighted that the older women are given the role of teachers. He notices in them a tiny spark that wasn't present before. Of course, his own return always interrupts whatever lesson is underway. On occasion he sits with them, listening, learning of a people and culture so different from his own. He often asks questions, which the women are pleased to answer—further educating the children, who seem more interested when Lale has asked the question. Having spent all his life in one home with his family, the nomadic existence of the Romany intrigues him. His life of comfort and knowing his place in the world, his education and life experiences seem mundane and predictable compared to the travels and struggles endured by the people he now finds himself living with. There is one woman he has often noticed on her own. She appears to have no children or family, no one who engages with her or shows her affection. Often she is just an extra pair of hands for a mother struggling with too many children. She looks like she's in her fifties, though Lale has learned that Romany men and women often look older than their years.

One evening after they have both assisted with getting the children to sleep, Lale follows her outside.

"Thank you for your help tonight," he begins.

She gives him a thin smile and sits on a pile of bricks to rest. "I've been putting children to bed since I was a baby myself. I could do it with my eyes closed."

Lale sits beside her. "I don't doubt it. But you don't seem to have any family here?"

She shakes her head sadly. "My husband and son died of typhus. It's only me now. Nadya."

"I'm so sorry, Nadya. I'd like to hear about them. My name is Lale."

That evening, Lale and Nadya converse long into the night. Lale does most of the talking, with Nadya preferring to listen. He tells her of his family back in Slovakia and of his love for

Gita. He discovers that Nadya is only forty-one years old. Her son had been six when he died three years ago, two days before his father. When Lale asks for her opinions, he finds Nadya's answers similar to those his mother would give. Is it this that draws him to her, that makes him want to protect her the way he wants to protect Gita? He finds himself sinking into an acute homesickness. He can't ignore his fears about the future. Dark thoughts he has kept at bay, about his family and their safety, consume him. If he can't help them, then he will do what he can for this woman in front of him.

A FEW DAYS LATER, AS HE ARRIVES BACK AT THE BLOCK, A YOUNG one toddles up to him. Lale sweeps him up in his arms. The boy's weight and smell remind him of the young nephew he said goodbye to more than a year ago. Overcome with emotion, Lale places the child back down and hurries inside. For once, none of the children follows him; something tells them to keep their distance.

Lying on his bed, he thinks back to the last time he was with his family. The farewell at the train station as he left for Prague. His mother had helped him pack his suitcase. In between wiping away tears, she kept taking out clothes he had packed and putting in books "for comfort and a reminder of home, wherever you end up."

As they stood on the platform, with Lale about to board the train, he saw tears in his father's eyes for the first time. He had expected them from everyone else, but not from his strong, dependable father. From his carriage window, he saw his father being helped away by his brother and sister. His mother ran the length of the platform, her arms outstretched, trying desperately to reach out to her baby boy. His two young nephews, oblivious to their changing world, ran innocently along the platform, chasing the train.

Clutching his suitcase, which contained only clothes and the few books he'd allowed his mother to pack, Lale leaned his head against the window and sobbed. He had been so caught up in his family's emotions that he hadn't registered his own devastating loss.

Chiding himself for letting his situation get to him, Lale goes back outside and chases the children around, letting them catch him and climb all over him. *Who needs trees when you have a Tätowierer to hang from?* That evening, he joins a group of men sitting outside. They share memories and stories of family life, captivated by the differences and similarities between their cultures. With the emotion of the day still running high, he says, "You know, in another life I would have had nothing to do with you. I would probably have turned away from you, or crossed the street if I saw you walking toward me."

There is silence for several moments before one of the men pipes up, "Hey, Tätowierer, in another life we would have had nothing to do with you, either. We would have crossed the street first."

The laughter that follows brings one of the women outside to tell them to be quiet—they will wake the children, and then there will be trouble. The men retreat inside, duly chastened. Lale lingers. He's not tired enough to sleep. He senses Nadya's presence and turns to see her standing in the doorway.

"Join me," he says.

Nadya sits beside him, staring off into the night. He studies her face in profile. She is quite beautiful. Her unshaven brown hair cascades down her shoulders and blows in the slight breeze around her face, so that she spends a good deal of time tucking it back behind her ears. A gesture so familiar to him, a gesture his mother made all day, every day, as wayward strands escaped from her tight bun or from under the scarf that hid it. Nadya speaks with the quietest natural voice he has ever heard. She's not whispering—this is her voice. Lale finally works out what it is about her voice that saddens him. It is emotionless. Whether she is relaying stories of happy times with her family or talking about the tragedy of being here, there is no change in her tone.

"What does your name mean?" he asks.

"Hope. It means hope." Nadya stands. "Good night," she says. She is gone before Lale can reply.

11

LALE AND LEON'S DAILY LIVES ARE STILL BEING DICTATED BY the arrival of transports from across Europe. As spring becomes summer, they do not stop coming.

Today the pair is working with long rows of female prisoners. The selection process is taking place a small distance away. They are too busy to pay attention to it. An arm and a piece of paper appear before them, and they do their job. Over and again. These prisoners are unusually quiet, perhaps sensing evil in the air. Lale suddenly hears someone break into a whistle. The tune is familiar, perhaps an opera. The whistling grows louder, and Lale glances in its direction. A man in a white coat is walking their way. Lale puts his head down, attempting to keep to the rhythm of his job. *Don't look at faces.* He takes the paper and makes the number, the same as he has a thousand times before.

The whistling stops. The doctor is now standing beside Lale, emitting a pungent smell of disinfectant. Leaning over, he inspects Lale's work and takes the arm he is midway through tattooing. He must be satisfied because he moves on as quickly as he arrived, bastardizing another melody. Lale looks up at Leon, who has turned pale. Baretski materializes beside them.

"What do you think of our new doctor?"

"Didn't really introduce himself," murmurs Lale.

Baretski laughs. "This is one doctor you don't want to be introduced to, trust me. *I'm* scared of him. The guy's a creep."

"Do you know what his name is?"

"Mengele, Herr Doktor Josef Mengele. You should remember that name, Tätowierer."

"What was he doing at the selection?"

"Herr Doktor has made it known that he will be at many of the selections, as he is looking for particular patients."

"I take it being sick is not a criterion for him."

Baretski doubles over laughing. "You can be so funny sometimes, Tätowierer."

⁓

LALE GOES BACK TO WORK. A LITTLE WHILE LATER HE HEARS the whistling start up behind him again, and the sound shoots such a shock of fear through his body that he slips and stabs the young woman he is tattooing. She cries out. Lale wipes the blood that trickles down her arm. Mengele steps closer.

"Something wrong, Tätowierer? You are the Tätowierer, are you not?" Mengele asks.

His voice sends chills down Lale's spine.

"Sir, I mean, yes, sir . . . I am the Tätowierer, Herr Doktor," Lale stammers.

Mengele, beside him now, stares him down, his eyes black as coal, devoid of compassion. A strange smile stretches across his face. Then he moves on.

Baretski approaches and punches Lale hard on the arm. "Having a hard day, Tätowierer? Perhaps you'd like to take a break and clear the latrines instead?"

❧

THAT NIGHT, LALE TRIES TO WASH THE DRIED BLOOD FROM HIS shirt with water from a puddle. He partially succeeds, but then decides that a stain will be an appropriate reminder of the day he met Mengele. A doctor who will cause more pain than he eases, Lale suspects; whose very existence threatens in ways Lale doesn't want to contemplate. Yes, a stain must remain to remind Lale of the new danger that has entered his life. He must always be wary of this man whose soul is colder than his scalpel.

❧

THE NEXT DAY, LALE AND LEON FIND THEMSELVES AT AUSCH-witz again, to number young women. The whistling doctor is present. He stands before the parade of girls, deciding their fate with a flick of his hand: *right, left, right, right, left, left*. Lale can't see any logic to the decisions. They are all in the prime of their lives, fit and healthy. He sees Mengele watching him. Lale can't take his eyes away as Mengele grabs the next girl's face in his big hands, twists it backward and forward and up and down, and opens her mouth. And then, with a slap to her face, he pushes her to the left. Rejected. Lale stares him down. Mengele calls an SS officer over and speaks to him. The officer looks over at Lale and begins walking in his direction. *Shit.*

"What do you want?" he demands with more confidence than he feels.

"Shut up, Tätowierer." The SS officer turns to Leon. "Leave your things and come with me."

"Wait a minute—you can't take him. Can't you see the number of people still to be done?" Lale asks, now terrified on his young assistant's behalf.

"Then you'd better get on with your work or you will be here all night, Tätowierer. And Herr Doktor won't like that."

"Leave him, please. Let us get on with our work. I'm sorry if I've done something to upset Herr Doktor," Lale says.

The officer points his rifle at Lale. "Do you want to come, too, Tätowierer?"

Leon says, "I'll go. It's OK, Lale. I'll be back as soon as I can."

"I'm sorry, Leon." Lale can no longer look at his friend.

"It's all right. I'll be all right. Get back to work."

Leon is marched off.

⌇

THAT EVENING LALE, GREATLY DISTRESSED, TRUDGES ALONE, head down, back to Birkenau. Something just off the track catches his eye, a flash of color. A flower, a single flower, waving in the breeze. Bloodred petals around a jet-black middle. He looks for others, but there are none. Still, it is a flower, and he wonders again about the next time he will be able to give flowers to someone he cares for. Images of Gita and his mother come to him, the two women he loves the most, floating just out of reach. Grief comes in waves, threatening to drown him. *Will the two ever meet? Will the younger learn from the older? Will Mama welcome and love Gita as I do?*

He had learned and practiced the art of flirting on his mother. Though he was fairly sure she didn't realize what he was doing, he knew; he knew what he was doing; he learned what worked on her and what didn't, and he quickly worked out what was appropriate and inappropriate behavior between a man and a woman. He suspected that all young men embarked on this learning process with their mothers, though he often wondered if they consciously realized it. He had brought it up with several of his friends, who had reacted with shock, claiming they did no such thing. When he questioned them further about whether they got away with more from their mother than their father, they all admitted to behaviors that could be construed as flirting—though they thought they were just getting around Mom because she was easier than Dad. Lale knew exactly what he was doing.

Lale's emotional connection to his mother had shaped the way he related to girls and women. He was attracted to all women, not just physically but emotionally. He loved talking to them; he loved making them feel good about themselves. To him, all women were beautiful and he believed there was no harm in telling them so. His mother and sister subliminally taught Lale what it was a woman wanted from a man, and so far he had spent his life trying to live up to these lessons. "Be attentive, Lale; remember the small things, and the big things will work themselves out." He heard his mother's sweet voice.

He bends and gently picks the short stem. He will find a

way to give it to Gita tomorrow. Back in his room, Lale carefully places the precious flower beside his bed before falling into a dreamless sleep, but the next morning when he wakes, the petals from his flower have separated and lie curled up beside the black center. *Death alone persists in this place.*

12

LALE DOESN'T WANT TO LOOK AT THE FLOWER ANYMORE, SO he leaves his block to throw it away. Baretski is there but Lale ignores him, preferring to head back inside and into his room. Baretski follows him and leans in the doorway. He studies the distraught-looking Lale. Lale is aware that he is sitting on a lumpy fortune of gems, currency, sausage, and chocolate. He grabs his bag and pushes past Baretski, forcing him to turn and follow him outside.

"Wait up, Tätowierer. I need to talk to you."

Lale stops.

"I have a request for you."

Lale remains silent, looking at a point beyond Baretski's shoulder.

"We—I mean my fellow officers and I—are in need of some entertainment, and as the weather is improving, we were thinking of a game of soccer. What do you think?"

"I'm sure it would be fun for you."

"Yes, indeed."

Baretski plays the game and waits.

Lale eventually blinks. "How can I help you?"

"Well, now that you've asked, Tätowierer, we need you to find eleven prisoners to take on a team of SS in a friendly match."

Lale considers laughing but keeps his gaze on a point over Baretski's shoulder. He thinks long and hard about his reply to this bizarre request.

"What, no substitutes?"

"No substitutes."

"Sure, why not." *Where did that come from? There are a million other things I could have said. Like, "Fuck off."*

"Good, great. Get your team together and we'll meet in the compound in two days' time—Sunday. Oh, and we'll bring the ball." Laughing loudly, Baretski walks off. "By the way, Tätowierer, you can have the day off. There are no transports today."

⟿

LALE SPENDS PART OF THE DAY SORTING HIS TREASURE INTO small bundles. Food for the Romany and the boys in Block 7, and of course for Gita and her friends. Gems and currency sorted by type. The process is surreal. Diamonds with diamonds, rubies with rubies, dollars with dollars, and even a stack of currency he has never seen before, bearing the words *South African Reserve Bank* and *Suid-Afrikaanse Reserwebank*. He has no idea of its value, or how it found its way into Birkenau. Taking several gems, he goes looking for Victor and Yuri to make the day's purchases. He then plays for a while with the boys from his block as he tries to formulate what he will say to the men in Block 7 upon their return from work.

In the evening, Lale is surrounded by dozens of men looking at him incredulously.

"You have got to be fucking kidding," one of them says.

"No," Lale replies.

"You want us to play soccer with the fucking SS?"

"Yes. This coming Sunday."

"Well, I'm not gonna do it. You can't make me," the same person replies.

From the back of the group, a voice calls out: "I'll play. I've played a little." A small man pushes his way through the gathered men and stands in front of Lale. "I'm Joel."

"Thanks, Joel. Welcome to the team. I need another nine of you. What have you got to lose? This is your one chance to get a little physical with the bastards and get away with it."

"I know a guy in Block 15 who played on the Hungarian national team, I'll ask him, if you like?" another prisoner pipes up.

"What about you?" Lale asks.

"Yeah, sure. I'm Joel, too. I'll ask around, see who I can get. Is there any chance we can have a practice before Sunday?"

"Plays soccer and has a sense of humor—I like this guy. I'll be back tomorrow night to see how you've done. Thanks, Big Joel." Lale looks over at the other Joel. "No offense."

"None taken," Little Joel replies.

Lale produces bread and sausage from his bag and lays it upon a nearby bunk. As he leaves, he watches two of the men share out the food. Each recipient breaks his portion into bite-size pieces and hands them around. No pushing, no fighting; an orderly distribution of life-saving nourishment. He overhears one man say,

"Here, Big Joel, you have mine—you'll need your energy." Lale smiles. A day that started badly is ending with a magnanimous gesture from a starving man.

⌒

THE DAY OF THE GAME ARRIVES. LALE WANDERS INTO THE main compound to see SS officers painting a white line into what is far from an oblong shape. He hears his name being called and finds his "team" gathered together. He joins the men.

"Hey, Lale, I've got fourteen players, counting you and me—a couple in reserve if some of us fall over," Big Joel tells him proudly.

"Sorry, I was told no substitutes. Just one team. Choose the fittest."

The men look at each other. Three hands rise, and those volunteering to take no part walk away. Lale watches as several of the men stretch and jump up and down in the manner of a professional warm-up.

"Some of these guys look like they know what they are doing," Lale mutters to Little Joel.

"They should. Six of them have played semiprofessionally."

"You're kidding!"

"Nope. We're gonna kick their asses."

"Little Joel, you can't. We can't win. I guess I didn't make myself clear."

"You said get a team together and Big Joel did."

"Yeah, but we can't win. We can't do anything to humiliate them. We can't tempt them to open fire on everyone. Look around you."

Little Joel sees the hundreds of prisoners gathered. There is an air of excitement in the camp as they push and shove for a vantage point around the perimeter of the painted playing area. He sighs. "I'll tell the others."

Lale scans the crowd for one face only. Gita is standing with her friends and waves to him furtively. He waves back, wanting desperately to run to her, sweep her up in his arms, and disappear behind the administration building. He hears loud banging and turns to see several SS pounding large poles in the ground at each end to make goalposts.

Baretski approaches him. "Come with me."

At one end of the field, the crowd of prisoners parts as the SS team enters. None of them is in uniform. Several wear clothing that will make playing a game of soccer much easier. Shorts, sleeveless shirts. Behind the team, a heavily guarded Schwarzhuber and Lale's boss, Houstek, approach Lale and Baretski.

"This is the captain of the prisoner team, the Tätowierer." Baretski introduces Lale to Schwarzhuber.

"Tätowierer." He turns to one of his guards. "Do we have something we can play for?"

A senior SS officer takes a cup from a soldier beside him and shows it to his commandant.

"We have this. I believe it will make a more than suitable trophy. The inscription says '1930 World Cup.' I believe the winners were France." He shows the trophy to Lale. "What do you think?"

Before Lale can respond, Schwarzhuber takes the trophy and holds it aloft for everyone to see. The SS cheer. "Start the game, and may the best team win."

As Lale jogs back to his team he mutters, "May the best team live to see the sun come up tomorrow."

Lale joins his team, and they gather in the middle of the field. The spectators cheer. The referee kicks the ball toward the SS team, and it's game on.

Ten minutes into the game, the prisoners have scored two goals to nil. While Lale enjoys the goals, common sense prevails when he looks at the angry faces of the SS. He subtly lets his players know to slow it down for the remainder of the half. They have had their moments of glory, and it is now time to let the SS into the game. The half ends two all. While the SS are given drinks during the short break, Lale and his team gather to discuss tactics. Eventually, Lale impresses on them that they cannot win this game. It is agreed that to help boost morale among the watching prisoners, two more goals can be scored, as long as they lose by one goal in the end.

As the second half begins, ash rains down on players and spectators. The core task of Birkenau has not been interrupted by sports. Another goal goes in for the prisoners, and another for the SS. As their appallingly inadequate diet begins to tell, the prisoners tire. The SS score two more goals. The prisoners don't need to throw the game; they simply can't compete any longer. With the SS two up, the referee blows his whistle for full time. Schwarzhuber makes his way onto the field and presents the trophy to the SS captain, who raises it aloft to muted cheers from the guards and officers present. As the SS make their way back to their barracks to celebrate, Houstek walks past Lale.

"Well played, Tätowierer."

Lale gathers his team and tells them what a great job they've done. The crowd has begun to disperse. He looks around to find Gita, who hasn't moved from her spot. He jogs over to her and takes her by the hand. They move through the other prisoners toward the administration block. As Gita drops to the ground behind the building, Lale looks around for prying eyes. Satisfied, he sits beside her. He watches Gita as she runs her fingers through the grass, examining it intently.

"What are you doing?"

"Looking for a four-leaf clover. You'd be surprised by how many there are here."

Lale smiles, charmed. "You're kidding."

"No, I've found several. Ivana finds them all the time. You look shocked."

"I am. You're the girl who doesn't believe she'll get out of here, yet you are looking for good-luck charms!"

"They're not for me. It's true I don't believe in such things."

"For who, then?"

"Do you know how superstitious the SS are? If we find a four-leaf clover, we treasure it. It's like currency for us."

"I don't understand."

"Whenever we are in danger from the SS, we hand it over. Sometimes it stops them from hitting us. If we take one to a meal, we might even get extra rations."

Lale gently strokes her face. That he cannot protect the girl he loves anguishes him greatly. Gita leans back down and continues her search. Grabbing a handful of grass, she throws it at Lale with a smile. He grins back. Playfully, he nudges her over and she lies on her back. Leaning over her, he plucks a handful of grass and slowly lets it sprinkle down onto her face. She blows it away. Another handful of grass goes onto her neck and the top of her chest. She leaves it there. He undoes the top button on her shirt, drops more grass, and watches it disappear down her cleavage.

"May I kiss you?" he asks.

"Why would you want to? I haven't brushed my teeth for I don't know how long."

"Me neither, so I guess we cancel each other out."

Gita answers him by raising her head toward him. Their previous fleeting kiss has ignited a year's worth of longing. Pent-up passions collide as they explore each other. They want, they need more of each other.

The moment is broken by the sound of a barking dog nearby. They know that the animal must have a handler attached to it. Lale stands and pulls Gita up into his arms. One last kiss before they run back to the safety of the compound and a crowd they can melt into.

In the women's camp, they spot Dana, Ivana, and Cilka and begin walking toward them.

Lale notices Cilka's pallor. "Is Cilka all right?" he asks. "She doesn't look well."

"She's as well as can be expected. Under the circumstances."

"Is she sick? Do you need medicine?"

"No, she's not sick. You're better off not knowing."

As they near the girls, Lale leans into Gita, whispering, "Tell me. Maybe I can help."

"Not this time, my love." Gita is encircled by the girls and they walk off. Cilka, head down, lags behind.

My love!

13

THAT NIGHT LALE LIES ON HIS BED, THE HAPPIEST HE'S BEEN for as long as he can remember.

In her own bed, Gita lies curled up next to a sleeping Dana, her eyes wide open, staring into the darkness, reliving the moments she lay with Lale: his kisses, the longing her body felt for him to continue, to go further. Her face grows hot as fantasies of their next encounter play out in her mind.

In a grand four-poster bed, Schwarzhuber and Cilka lie in each other's arms. His hands explore her body as she stares into nothing, feeling nothing. Numb.

In his private dining room at Auschwitz, Hoess sits at an elegant table for one. Fine food rests on fine china. He pours 1932 Château Latour into a crystal goblet. He swirls, sniffs, tastes the wine. He won't let the stresses and strains of his job impede life's little luxuries.

A drunken Baretski stumbles into his room in the barracks

at Auschwitz. Kicking the door shut, he staggers and falls awkwardly onto his bed. With difficulty, he removes the belt holding his sidearm and slings it over the bedpost. Sprawled on his bed, he registers the overhead light—still on, shining into his eyes. After an unsuccessful attempt to get up, he locates his weapon with a clumsy arm and pulls it from its holster. With his second shot, he kills the recalcitrant light bulb. His gun drops to the floor as he passes out.

⁂

THE NEXT MORNING, LALE WINKS AT GITA AS HE COLLECTS HIS supplies and instructions from Bella in the administration office. His smile disappears when he notices Cilka sitting beside Gita, her head down, once again not acknowledging him. *This has been going on far too long.* He resolves to force Gita to tell him what is wrong with Cilka. Outside, he is met by a very hungover, angry Baretski.

"Hurry up. I've got a truck waiting to take us to Auschwitz."

Lale follows him to the truck. Baretski climbs into the cab, shutting the door. Lale gets the message and scrambles into the back. There he endures the trip to Auschwitz, tossed from one side to the other.

When they arrive at Auschwitz, Baretski tells Lale that he is going to lie down and that Lale is to make his way to Block 10. Once he finds the block, Lale is directed to the back by the SS officer standing out front. Lale notices that it looks different from the blocks back at Birkenau.

The first thing he sees as he rounds the corner of the building is the wire fence that encloses part of the yard. Slowly, he registers small movements in the enclosed area. He stumbles forward, transfixed at what lies beyond the fence: girls, dozens of them, naked—many lying down, some sitting, some standing, hardly any of them moving. Paralyzed, Lale watches as a guard comes into the enclosure and walks through the girls, picking up their left arms, looking for a number, possibly one made by Lale. Finding the girl he wants, the guard drags her through the bodies. Lale looks at the girls' faces. Vacant. Silent. He notices several leaning against the wire fence. Unlike the other fences at Auschwitz and Birkenau, this one is not electrified. The option of self-destruction has been taken from them.

"Who are you?" a voice behind him demands.

Lale turns. An SS officer has come out from a back door. Slowly Lale holds up his bag.

"Tätowierer."

"So what are you standing out here for? Get inside."

One or two of the doctors and nurses in white coats greet him cursorily as he walks through a large room toward a desk. The prisoners here don't look like people. More like marionettes abandoned by their puppeteers. He approaches the nurse sitting behind the desk and holds up his bag.

"Tätowierer."

She looks at him with disgust, sneers, stands, and walks off. He follows her. She leads him down a long corridor and into a large room. About fifty young women stand there in a line. Silent. The room smells sour. At the front of the line, Mengele is examining one of the girls, roughly opening her mouth, grasping her hips, then her breasts, as tears fall silently down her face. Finishing his examination, he waves her off to the right. Rejected. Another girl is pushed into her vacated place.

The nurse walks Lale up to Mengele, who stops his examination. "You are late," he says with a smirk, clearly enjoying Lale's discomfort. He indicates a small group of girls standing to his left.

"'Those I am keeping. Do their numbers."

Lale moves off.

"One day soon, Tätowierer, I will take you."

Lale looks back, and there it is. That tight pull of the lips that constitutes a sick smile. Once again, a chill spreads throughout his body. His hands shake. Lale picks up his pace, hurrying to a small table where another nurse sits with identification cards at the ready. She makes room for him to set up. He tries to control the shaking in his hands as he lines up his tools and ink bottles. He looks over at Mengele, who has another frightened girl in front of him. He runs his hands over her hair and down her breasts.

"Don't be frightened, I'm not going to hurt you," Lale hears him tell her.

Lale watches the girl shiver in fear.

"There, there. You're safe, this is a hospital. We take care of people here."

Mengele turns to a nearby nurse. "Get a blanket for this pretty young thing."

Turning back to the girl, he says, "I'll take good care of you."

The girl is sent in Lale's direction. Lale puts his head down and prepares to get into the rhythm of tattooing the numbers shown to him by the nurse assisting.

When his work is complete, Lale leaves the building and looks again into the fenced area. It is empty. He drops to his knees and dry retches. He has nothing to bring up; the only fluid in his body is tears.

～

THAT NIGHT, GITA RETURNS TO HER BLOCK TO LEARN THAT there are several new arrivals. The established residents eye the newcomers with resentment. They don't want to have to talk about the horrors that lie in store, nor share their rations.

"Gita. Is that you, Gita?" a feeble voice calls out.

Gita approaches the group of women, many of whom seem older. Older women are rarely seen in Birkenau, which is home to the young who can work. A woman steps forward, her arms outstretched. "Gita, it is me, your neighbor Hilda Goldstein."

Gita stares and suddenly recognizes a neighbor from her hometown of Vranov nad Topl'ou, paler and thinner than when Gita saw her last.

Memories flood Gita, scents and textures and flashes of the past: a familiar doorway, the aroma of chicken soup, a cracked bar of soap by the kitchen sink, happy voices on warm summer nights, her mother's arms.

"Mrs. Goldstein . . ." Gita moves closer, clasps the woman's hand. "They took you, too."

The woman nods. "They took us all away maybe a week ago. I got separated from the others and put on a train."

A rush of hope. "My parents and sisters are with you?"

"No, they took them several months ago. Your parents and your sisters. Your brothers have been gone for a long time—your mother said they joined the resistance."

"Do you know where they were taken?"

Mrs. Goldstein drops her head. "I'm sorry. We were told they were . . . They were . . ."

Gita crumbles to the floor as Dana and Ivana rush to her, sit on the ground, and embrace her. Above them, Mrs. Goldstein continues to speak: "I'm sorry, I'm sorry." Both Dana and Ivana are crying, holding the dry-eyed Gita. They babble words of condolence at Gita. *Gone.* No memories come now. She feels a terrible emptiness inside her. She turns to her friends and asks in a halting, broken voice, "Do you think maybe it's OK for me to cry? Just a little bit?"

"Do you want us to pray with you?" asks Dana.

"No, just a few tears. That's all I'll let these murderers have from me."

Ivana and Dana both wipe their own tears with the backs of their sleeves as silent tears begin to roll down Gita's face. They take turns wiping them away. Finding a strength she didn't know she possessed, Gita stands and embraces Mrs. Goldstein. Around her she can feel the recognition of those witnessing her moment of grief. They look on in silence, each going into their own dark place of despair, not knowing what has become of their own families. Slowly, the two groups of women—the longtimers and the newcomers—join together.

AFTER SUPPER, GITA SITS WITH MRS. GOLDSTEIN, WHO BRINGS her up-to-date on events back home: how, slowly, family by family, it was torn apart. Stories had filtered back about the concentration camps. No one quite knew that they had been turned into production lines of death. But they knew that people were not coming back. And yet only a few had left their homes to seek a safe haven in a neighboring country. It becomes obvious to Gita that Mrs. Goldstein will not survive long if she is made to labor here. She is older than her years—physically and emotionally broken.

The next morning, Gita approaches their kapo to ask for a favor. She will ask Lale to try to get the kapo anything she wants if Mrs. Goldstein can be spared hard work and spend the day in the block. She suggests that Mrs. Goldstein empty the toilet buckets each night, a task usually given to a person chosen each day by the kapo, often someone she believes has spoken badly of her. The kapo's price is a diamond ring. She's heard the rumors of Lale's treasure chest. The deal is struck.

          ⌇

FOR THE NEXT SEVERAL WEEKS, LALE GOES TO AUSCHWITZ every day. The five crematoria are working at full capacity, but large numbers of prisoners still have to be tattooed. He receives his instructions and supplies from the administration building at Auschwitz. He has no time and no need to go to the administration building at Birkenau, so he has no opportunity to see Gita. He wants to get a message to her that he is safe.

Baretski is in a good, even playful mood—he has a secret and wants Lale to guess what it might be. Lale plays Baretski's juvenile game.

"You're letting us all go home?"

Baretski laughs and punches Lale on the arm.

"You've been promoted?"

"You'd better hope not, Tätowierer. Otherwise, someone not as nice as me will end up minding you."

"OK, I give up."

"I'll tell you, then. You're all going to be given extra rations and blankets next week for a few days. The Red Cross are coming to inspect your holiday camp."

Lale thinks hard. *What can this mean? Will the outside world finally see what is happening here?* He works to keep his emotions in check in front of Baretski.

"That will be nice. Do you think this camp will pass the humanitarian test of imprisonment?"

Lale can see Baretski's brain ticking, almost hear the little clicks. He finds his lack of comprehension amusing, though he doesn't dare smile.

"You'll be well-fed for the days they are here—well, those of you we let them see."

"So it will be a controlled visit?"

"Do you think we're stupid?" Baretski laughs.

Lale lets that question pass.

"Can I ask a favor?"

"You can ask," says Baretski.

"If I write a note to Gita telling her I'm OK and just busy at Auschwitz, will you get it to her?"

"I'll do better. I'll tell her myself."

"Thank you."

Although Lale and a select group of prisoners do receive some extra rations for a few days, they soon dry up and Lale is unsure if the Red Cross ever did enter the camp. Baretski is more than capable of making up the whole idea. Lale has to trust that his message to Gita will be conveyed—though he doesn't trust Baretski to do it straightforwardly. He can only wait and hope that a Sunday when he doesn't have to work will arrive soon.

FINALLY THE DAY COMES WHEN LALE FINISHES WORK EARLY. He races between the camps and gets to the Birkenau administration building just as the workers are leaving. Impatiently, he waits. Why does she have to be one of the last ones out today? At last she appears. Lale's heart leaps. He wastes no time grabbing her by the arm and taking her to the back of the building. She trembles as he pushes her up against the wall.

"I thought you were dead. I thought I'd never see you again. I . . ." she stammers.

He runs his hands along her face. "Did you not get my message from Baretski?"

"No. I got no message from anyone."

"Shh, it's OK," he says. "I've been at Auschwitz every day for weeks."

"I was so frightened."

"I know. But I'm here now. And I have something to say to you."

"What?"

"First, let me kiss you."

They kiss, clutching, pressing, passionately, before she pushes him away.

"What do you want to say?"

"My beautiful Gita. You've bewitched me. I've fallen in love with you."

They feel like words he's waited all his life to say.

"Why? Why would you say that? Look at me. I'm ugly, I'm dirty. My hair . . . I used to have lovely hair."

"I love your hair the way it is now, and I will love it the way it will be in the future."

"But we have no future."

Lale holds her firmly around her waist, forces her to meet his gaze.

"Yes, we do. There will be a tomorrow for us. On the night I arrived here, I made a vow to myself that I would survive this hell. We will survive and make a life where we are free to kiss when we want to, make love when we want to."

Gita blushes and turns away. He gently moves her face back to him.

"To be free to make love wherever, whenever we want to. Do you hear me?"

Gita nods.

"Do you believe me?"

"I want to, but—"

"No buts. Just believe me. Now you'd better get back to your block before your kapo starts wondering."

As Lale begins to walk off, Gita pulls him back and kisses him hard.

Breaking the kiss, he says, "Maybe I should stay away more often."

"Don't you dare," she says, hitting him in the chest.

&

THAT NIGHT IVANA AND DANA PEPPER GITA WITH QUESTIONS, relieved to see their friend smiling again.

"Did you tell him about your family?" asks Dana.

"No."

"Why not?"

"I can't. It's too painful to talk about . . . and he was so happy to see me."

"Gita, if he loves you as he says he does, he would want to know that you have lost your family. He would want to comfort you."

"You might be right, Dana, but if I tell him, then we'll both be sad, and I want our time together to be different. I want to forget where I am and what's happened to my family. And when he holds me in his arms, I do forget, just for those few brief moments. Is it wrong of me to want to escape reality for a bit?"

"No, not at all."

"I'm sorry that I have my escape, my Lale. You know I wish with all my heart the same for you two."

"We are very happy that you have him," says Ivana.

"It is enough that one of us has a little happiness. We share in it, and you let us—that's enough for us," says Dana.

"Just don't keep any secrets from us, all right?" says Ivana.

"No secrets," says Gita.

"No secrets," agrees Dana.

14

THE NEXT MORNING, LALE APPEARS IN THE ADMINISTRATION office and approaches Bella at the main desk.

"Lale, where have you been?" Bella says with a warm smile. "We thought something had happened to you."

"Auschwitz."

"Ah, say no more. You must be low on supplies—wait here and I'll stock you up."

"Not too much, Bella."

Bella looks over at Gita. "Of course. We need to make sure you come back tomorrow."

"You know me too well, young Bella. Thank you."

Bella wanders off to get his supplies, and Lale leans on the desk and stares at Gita. He knows she has seen him come in but is playing coy and keeping her head down. She runs a finger over her lips. Lale aches with desire.

He also notices that the chair next to her, Cilka's, is empty. Again he tells himself to find out what is happening with her.

He leaves the office and heads over to the selection area, having already noted that a truck has arrived with new prisoners. As he is setting up his table, Baretski appears.

"I've got someone here to see you, Tätowierer."

Before Lale can look up, he hears a familiar voice, no more than a whisper.

"Hello, Lale."

Leon stands beside Baretski—pale, thinner, stooped, carefully placing one foot in front of the other.

"I'll leave you two to get reacquainted." A smiling Baretski walks off.

"Leon, oh my god, you're alive." Lale rushes to embrace him. He can feel every bone through his friend's shirt. He holds him at arm's length, examining him. "Mengele. Was it Mengele?"

Leon can only nod. Lale gently runs his hands down Leon's skinny arms, touches his face.

"The bastard. One day he'll get his. As soon as I've finished here, I can get you plenty of food. Chocolate, sausage, what do you want? I'll fatten you up."

Leon smiles weakly at him. "Thanks, Lale."

"I knew the bastard was starving prisoners. I thought he was only doing it to girls."

"If only that was all it was."

"What do you mean?"

Now Leon stares directly into Lale's eyes. "He cut my fucking balls off, Lale," he says, his voice strong and steady. "Somehow you lose your appetite when they cut your balls off."

Lale reels back in horror and turns away, not wanting Leon

to see his shock. Leon fights back a sob and struggles to find his voice as he searches the ground for something to focus on.

"I'm sorry, I shouldn't have said it like that. Thank you for your offer. I am grateful to you."

Lale breathes deeply, trying to control his anger. He badly wants to lash out, to take revenge for the crime committed against his friend.

Leon clears his throat. "Any chance I can have my job back?"

Lale's face floods with warmth. "Of course. Glad to have you back—but only when you've regained your strength," he says. "Why don't you go back to my room? If any of the Gypsies stop you, tell them you're my friend and I've sent you there. You'll find supplies under my bed. I'll see you when I'm done here."

A senior SS officer approaches.

"Go now, hurry."

"Hurrying is not something I can do right now."

"I'm sorry."

"It's OK. I'm gone. See you later."

The officer watches Leon walk off and turns back to what he was doing previously: determining who should live and die.

❧

THE NEXT DAY, LALE REPORTS TO THE ADMINISTRATION OF-fice and is told that he has the day off. No transports are arriving at either Auschwitz or Birkenau, and there is no request from Herr Doktor to assist him. He spends the morning with Leon. He'd bribed his old kapo in Block 7 to take Leon in, on the understanding that he will work for him when he has regained his strength. He gives him food that he had been planning to give to his Romany friends and to Gita for distribution.

As Lale is leaving Leon, Baretski calls out to him. "Tätowierer, where have you been? I have been looking for you."

"I was told I had the day off."

"Well, you don't anymore. Come, we have a job."

"I have to get my bag."

"You don't need your tools for this job. Come."

Lale hurries after Baretski. They are heading toward one of the crematoria.

He catches up with him. "Where are we going?"

"Are you worried?" Baretski laughs.

"Wouldn't you be?"

"No."

Lale's chest tightens; his breath comes too short. Should he run? If he does, Baretski will surely turn his weapon on him. But then, what would it matter? A bullet is surely preferable to the ovens.

They are very close to Crematorium 3 before Baretski decides to put Lale out of his misery. He slows his long strides.

"Don't worry. Now come on before we both get into trouble and end up in the ovens."

"You're not getting rid of me?"

"Not just yet. There are two prisoners in here who appear to have the same number. We need you to look at them. It must have been you or that eunuch who made the marks. You have to tell us which one is which."

The redbrick building looms in front of them; large windows disguise its purpose, but the size of the chimneys confirms its horrifying true nature. They are met at the entrance by two SS, who joke with Baretski and ignore Lale. They point to closed doors inside the building, and Baretski and Lale walk toward them. Lale looks around at this final stretch of the road to death at Birkenau.

He sees the Sonderkommando standing by, defeated, ready to do a job no one on earth would volunteer for: removing corpses from the gas chambers and putting them into the ovens. He tries to make eye contact with them, to let them know he, too, works for the enemy. He, too, has chosen to stay alive for as long as he can, by performing an act of defilement on people of his own faith. None of them meets his eye. He has heard what other prisoners say about these men and the privileged position they occupy—they are housed separately, receive extra rations, and have warm clothing and blankets to sleep under. Their lives parallel his, and he feels a sinking in his gut at the thought that he, too, is despised for the role he plays at the camp. Unable to express in any way his solidarity with these men, he walks on.

They are led to a large steel door. In front of it stands a guard.

"It's all right, all the gas is gone. We need to send them to the ovens, but we can't until you identify the correct numbers."

The guard opens the door for Lale and Baretski. Pulling himself up to his full height, Lale looks Baretski in the eye and sweeps his hand from left to right.

"After you."

Baretski bursts out laughing and slaps Lale on the back. "No, after you."

"No, after you," Lale repeats.

"I insist, Tätowierer."

The SS officer opens the doors wide and they step into a cavernous room. Bodies, hundreds of naked bodies, fill the room. They are piled up on each other, their limbs distorted. Dead eyes stare. Men, young and old; children at the bottom. Blood, vomit, urine, and feces. The smell of death pervades the entire space. Lale tries to hold his breath. His lungs burn. His legs threaten to give way beneath him. Behind him, Baretski says, "Shit."

That one word from a sadist only deepens the well of inhumanity that Lale is drowning in.

"Over here," an officer indicates, and they follow him to one side of the room, where two male bodies are laid out together. The officer starts talking to Baretski. For once, words fail him, and he indicates that Lale can understand German.

"They both have the same number. How could that be?" he asks.

Lale can only shake his head and shrug his shoulders. *How the hell should I know?*

"Look at them. Which one is correct?" the officer snaps.

Lale leans down and takes hold of one of the arms. He is grateful for a reason to kneel and hopes it will stabilize him. He looks closely at the numbers tattooed on the arm he holds.

"The other?" he asks.

Roughly, the other man's arm is thrust at him. He looks closely at both numbers.

"See, here. This is not a three, it's an eight. Part of it is faded, but it's an eight."

The guard scribbles on each cold arm the correct numbers. Without asking for permission, Lale gets up and leaves the crematorium. Baretski catches up with him outside, where he is doubled over and breathing deeply.

Baretski waits a moment or two.

"Are you all right?"

"No, I'm not fucking all right. You *bastards*. How many more of us must you kill?"

"You're upset. I can see that."

Baretski is just a kid, an uneducated kid. But Lale can't help wondering how he can feel nothing for the people they have just seen, the agony of death inscribed on their faces and twisted bodies.

"Come on, let's go," says Baretski.

Lale pulls himself up to walk beside him, though he cannot look at him.

"You know something, Tätowierer? I bet you're the only Jew who ever walked into an oven and then walked back out of it."

He laughs loudly, slaps Lale on the back, and strides off ahead.

15

LALE WALKS DETERMINEDLY FROM HIS BLOCK AND ACROSS THE compound. Two SS officers approach him, rifles at the ready. Without breaking step, he holds up his bag.

"Politische Abteilung!"

The rifles lower and he passes without another word. Lale enters the women's camp and heads immediately to Block 29, where he is met by the kapo, who is leaning against the building looking bored. Her charges are away working. She doesn't bother to move as he approaches her and takes from his bag a large block of chocolate. Having been warned by Baretski not to interfere in the relationship between the Tätowierer and prisoner 34902, she accepts the bribe.

"Please bring Gita to me. I'll wait inside."

Stuffing the chocolate down her ample bosom and shrugging her shoulders, the kapo sets off to the administration building. Lale goes inside the barracks block, shutting the door behind him.

He doesn't have to wait long. A flash of sunlight as the door opens tells him she has arrived. Gita sees him standing in the semi-darkness, his head bowed.

"You!"

Lale takes a step toward her. She steps back, hard up against the shut door, clearly distressed.

"Are you all right? Gita, it's me."

He takes one step closer and is shocked by her visible trembling.

"Say something, Gita."

"You . . . you . . ." she repeats.

"Yes, it's me, Lale." He takes hold of her two wrists and tries to hold them tightly.

"Do you have any idea what goes through your head when the SS come for you? Any idea at all?"

"Gita—"

"How could you? How could you let the SS take me?"

Lale is dumbfounded. He relaxes his grip on her wrists, and she pulls free and turns away.

"I'm sorry, I didn't mean to frighten you. I just asked your kapo to have you brought here. I needed to see you."

"When someone is taken away by the SS, they are never seen again. Do you understand? I thought I was being taken to die, and all I could think of was you. Not that I might never see my friends again, not Cilka who watched me go and who must be so upset, but that I would never see you. And here you are."

Lale is ashamed. His selfish need has caused his beloved this distress. Suddenly she runs at him with her fists raised. He reaches out to her as she crashes into him. She strikes him in the chest, and tears stream down her face. Lale takes the hits until they subside. Then, slowly, he lifts her face, wiping away tears with his hand and attempting to kiss her. As their lips meet, Gita pulls away, glaring at him. He holds out his arms for her to come back to him. Seeing her reluctance, he lowers them. She runs at him again, this time knocking him back against a wall as she tries to tear his shirt off. Stunned, Lale holds her at arm's length, but she will have none of it and pushes herself hard against him, kissing him violently. He lifts her by her bottom and she wraps her legs around his waist, kissing him so hungrily that she bites his lips. Lale tastes the salt of blood but kisses her back and stumbles onto a nearby bunk, where they tumble down together, tearing at each other's clothes. Their lovemaking is passionate, desperate. It is a need so long in the making that it cannot be denied. Two people desperate for the love and intimacy they fear they will otherwise never experience. It seals their commitment to each other, and Lale knows at this moment that he can love no other. It strengthens his resolve to go on another day, and another day, for a thousand days, for however long it takes for them to live by his words to Gita: "To be free to make love wherever, whenever we want to."

Exhausted, they lie in each other's arms. Gita falls asleep and Lale spends a long time just looking at her. The physical fight between them is over, replaced by a raging tumult within Lale. *What has this place done to us? What has it made us become? How much longer can we go on? She thought it was all ending today. I caused that pain. I must never do that again.*

He touches his lip. Winces. It breaks his dark mood and he smiles at the thought of where the pain has come from. He gently kisses Gita awake.

"Hi there," he whispers.

Gita rolls onto her stomach and looks at him, troubled. "Are you all right? You looked, I don't know . . . Even though I was upset when I came in, now that I think about it, you looked terrible."

Lale closes his eyes, sighing deeply.

"What happened?"

"Let's just say I took another step into the abyss but got to step back out of it."

"Will you tell me one day?"

"Probably not. Don't push it, Gita."

She nods.

"Now I think you'd better go back to the office so Cilka and the others can see that you're OK."

"Mmmm. I want to stay here with you, forever."

"Forever is a long time."

"Or it could be tomorrow," she says.

"No, it won't be."

Gita turns her head away, blushing, closing her eyes.

"What are you thinking?" he asks.

"I'm listening. To the walls."

"What are they saying?"

"Nothing. They're breathing heavily, weeping for those who leave here in the morning and do not return at night."

"They are not weeping for you, my love."

"Not today. I know that now."

"Or tomorrow. They will never weep for you. Now, get out of here and get back to work."

She curls into a ball. "Can you go first? I need to find my clothes."

After one last kiss, Lale scrambles around for his clothes. Dressed, he gives her another quick kiss before leaving. Outside the block, the kapo is back in her position against the wall.

"Feeling better, Tätowierer?"

"Yes, thanks."

"The chocolate is lovely. I like sausage, too."

"I'll see what I can do."

"You do that, Tätowierer. See you."

16

THE KNOCK ON HIS DOOR WAKES LALE FROM A DEEP SLEEP. HE opens up gingerly, half expecting to see one of the Romany boys. But two young men stand in the doorway, glancing this way and that, clearly frightened.

"What do you want?" Lale asks.

"Are you the Tätowierer?" one of them asks in Polish.

"Depends who's asking."

"We need the Tätowierer. We were told he lived here," says the other boy.

"Get in here before you wake the babies."

Lale shuts the door behind the boys and indicates for them to sit on the bed. They are both tall and skinny, and one has a smattering of freckles.

"I'll ask again, what do you want?"

"We have a friend—" the freckled boy stammers.

"Don't we all?" Lale interrupts.

"Our friend is in trouble—"

"Aren't we all?"

The two boys look at each other, trying to decide whether to continue.

"I'm sorry. Go on."

"He got caught, and we're scared they're going to kill him."

"Caught doing what?"

"Well, he escaped last week and they caught him and brought him back here. What do you think they're going to do to him?"

Lale is incredulous.

"How the hell did he escape, and how was he then stupid enough to get caught?"

"We're not sure of the full story."

"Well, he'll be hanged, probably first thing tomorrow morning. You know that's the punishment for trying to escape."

"Can you do anything? People say you can help."

"I can help if you want some extra food, but that's about it. Where is the boy right now?"

"He's outside."

"Outside this building?"

"Yeah."

"For god's sake, get him in here at once," Lale says, opening the door.

One of the boys hurries outside and soon returns with a young man, head bowed, shivering with fear. Lale points to the bed and he sits. His eyes are puffy.

"Your friends tell me you escaped."

"Yes, sir."

"How did you do that?"

"Well, I was working outside and I asked the guard if I could take a crap. He told me to go into the trees because he didn't want to smell it. Then when I went to return to my detail, they were all walking off. I was worried if I ran after them I might get shot by one of the other guards, so I just walked back into the forest."

"And?" asked Lale.

"Well, I kept walking. Then I got caught when I went into a village to steal some food. I was starving. The soldiers saw my tattooed number and brought me back here."

"And now they're going to hang you tomorrow morning, right?"

The boy's head drops. Lale reflects that this is how he will look tomorrow when the life has been strangled from him.

"Is there anything you can do to help us, Tätowierer?"

Lale paces his small room. He pulls up the boy's sleeve and studies his number. *One of mine.* He returns to pacing. The boys sit silently.

"Stay here," he says firmly, grabs his bag, and hurries from the room.

Searchlights scan the compound outside, as do violent eyes looking for someone to kill. Hugging buildings, Lale makes his way to the administration block and enters the main office. He is instantly relieved to see Bella behind the desk. She looks up at him.

"Lale, what are you doing here? I have no work for you."

"Hi, Bella. Can I ask you something?"

"Sure, anything. You know that, Lale."

"When I was here earlier today, did I hear talk of a transport going out tonight?"

"Yes, there's one leaving for another camp at midnight."

"How many on it?"

Bella picks up a sheet nearby. "One hundred names. Why?"

"Names, not numbers?"

"No, they're not numbered. They only arrived earlier today and are being sent to a boys' camp. No one is numbered there."

"Can we squeeze one more onto that list?"

"I guess so. Who? You?"

"No, you know I'm not leaving here without Gita. It's someone else—the less you know, the better."

"All right, I'll do that for you. What's his name?"

"Shit," Lale says. "I'll be right back."

Furious with himself, Lale makes haste back to his room. "Your name—what's your name?"

"Mendel."

"Mendel what?"

"Sorry, Mendel Bauer."

⊱⊰

BACK AT THE OFFICE, BELLA ADDS TO THE BOTTOM OF THE typed list.

"Won't the guards question a name not typed like the others?" Lale asks.

"No, they're too lazy to question that. It would create too much trouble for them to get involved. Just tell whoever it is to be in the compound when he sees the truck being loaded up."

From his bag, Lale takes a ring encrusted with rubies and diamonds and hands it to Bella. "Thank you. This is for you. You can either keep it or sell it. I'll make sure he is at the transport."

BACK IN HIS ROOM, LALE SWEEPS MENDEL'S TWO FRIENDS OFF the bed, takes out his bag, and sits down beside him.

"Give me your arm."

As the boys look on, Lale sets about changing the number into a snake. The job isn't perfect, but it's good enough to conceal the numbers.

"Why are you doing this?" one of the boys asks.

"Where Mendel is going, no one is numbered. It wouldn't take long for his number to be seen, and then he would be right back here, to keep his appointment with the hangman."

He finishes the job and turns to the two boys looking on.

"You two get back to your block now, and go carefully. I'm only good for one rescue per night," he says. "Your friend won't be here tomorrow. He's going out on a transport at midnight. I don't know where he's going, but wherever it is, he will have at least a chance of staying alive. Do you understand?"

The three boys hug and make promises to catch up on the other side of this nightmare. When the friends have gone, Lale sits back down beside Mendel.

"You'll stay here until it's time to go. I'll take you to the transport, and then you're on your own."

"I don't know how to thank you."

"If you manage to escape again, don't get caught. That will be thanks enough for me."

A short while later, Lale hears the telltale sounds of movement in the compound.

"Come on, time to go."

Sneaking out, they edge along the walls of the building until they can see two trucks with men being loaded on.

"Move quickly and try to get into the middle of one of the lines. Push your way in and give them your name when asked."

Mendel hurries off and manages to get in a line. He wraps his arms around himself to ward off the cold, and to protect the snake he now bears. Lale watches as the guard finds his name and ushers him on board. As the engine starts up and the truck moves off, Lale slinks back to his room.

17

THE MONTHS THAT FOLLOW ARE PARTICULARLY HARSH. PRISoners die in all manner of ways. Many are taken by disease, malnutrition, and exposure to the cold. A few make it to an electrified fence, killing themselves. Others are shot by a tower guard before they can. The gas chambers and crematoria are also working overtime, and Lale and Leon's tattooing stations teem with people as tens of thousands are transported to Auschwitz and Birkenau.

Lale and Gita see each other on Sundays when possible. On those days they mingle among other bodies, sneaking touches. Occasionally they can steal time together alone in Gita's block. This keeps them committed to staying alive and, in Lale's case, planning a shared future. Gita's kapo is getting fat from the food Lale brings her. On occasion, when Lale is prevented from seeing Gita for an extended period, she asks Gita outright, "When's your boyfriend coming next?"

On one Sunday, Gita finally, after repeated requests, tells Lale what is going on with Cilka. "Cilka is the plaything of Schwarzhuber."

"Oh, god. For how long has it been going on?"

"I don't know exactly. A year, maybe more."

"He's nothing more than a drunken, sadistic bastard," Lale says, clenching his fists. "I can only imagine how he treats her."

"Don't say that! I don't want to think about it."

"What does she tell you about their time together?"

"Nothing. We don't ask. I don't know how to help her."

"He'll kill her himself if she rejects him in any way. I suspect Cilka's already worked that out, otherwise she would have been dead long ago. Getting pregnant is the biggest worry."

"It's all right, no one is going to get pregnant. You have to be, you know, having your monthly cycle for that to happen. Didn't you know that?"

An embarrassed Lale says, "Well, yes, I knew that. It's just that it's not something we've talked about. I guess I didn't think."

"Neither you nor that sadistic bastard need to worry about Cilka or me having a baby. OK?"

"Don't compare me to him. Tell her I think she's a hero and I'm proud to say I know her."

"What do you mean, hero? She's not a hero," Gita says with some annoyance. "She just wants to live."

"And that makes her a hero. You're a hero, too, my darling. That the two of you have chosen to survive is a type of resistance to these Nazi bastards. Choosing to live is an act of defiance, a form of heroism."

"What does that make you?"

"I have been given the choice of participating in the destruction of our people, and I have chosen to do so in order to survive.

I can only hope I am not one day judged a perpetrator or a collaborator."

Gita leans over and kisses him. "You are a hero to me."

Time has run on, and they are startled when other girls start returning to the block. They are fully clothed, and so Lale's exit is not as embarrassing as it might otherwise have been.

"Hello. Hi. Dana, lovely to see you. Girls. Ladies," he says as he leaves.

The kapo, in her normal position at the entrance to the building, shakes her head at Lale.

"You need to be out of here when the others return. OK, Tätowierer?"

"Sorry, won't happen again."

Lale moves around the compound with half a spring in his step. He is surprised when he hears his name and looks around to see who is calling him. It is Victor. He and the other Polish workers are heading out of the camp. Victor summons him over.

"Hi, Victor. Yuri. How are you doing?"

"Not as good as you, by the look of it. What's going on?"

Lale waves his hand. "Nothing, nothing."

"We have supplies for you and thought we wouldn't be able to hand them over. Do you have room in your bag?"

"Absolutely. Sorry, I should've come and seen you sooner, but I, er, was busy."

Lale opens his bag, and Victor and Yuri fill it. There is too much to fit in.

"Do you want me to bring the rest back tomorrow?" Victor asks.

"No, I'll take it now, thanks. I'll see you tomorrow with payment."

There is one girl besides Cilka, among the tens of thousands in Birkenau, whom the SS have let keep her hair long. She is about Gita's age. Lale has never spoken to her, but he has seen her from time to time. She stands out, with her flowing blond mane. Everybody else tries as best they can to hide their cropped heads beneath a scarf, often torn from their shirt. Lale had asked Baretski one day what the deal was with her. How is she permitted to keep her hair long?

"On the day she came into the camp," Baretski answered, "Commandant Hoess was at the selections. He saw her, thought she was quite beautiful, and said her hair was not to be touched."

Lale has often been astounded by the things he has seen in both camps, but for Hoess to think only one girl is beautiful, out of the hundreds of thousands who have come through, truly confounds him.

As Lale hurries back to his room with a sausage shoved down his pants, he turns a corner and there she is, the "only" beautiful girl in the camp, staring at him. He makes it back to his room in record time.

18

SPRING HAS CHASED AWAY THE BITTEREST DEMONS OF WINter. The warmer weather offers a ray of hope to everyone who has survived the elements, along with their captors' cruel whims. Even Baretski is behaving less callously.

"I know you can get things, Tätowierer," he says, his voice lower than usual.

"I don't know what you mean," says Lale.

"Things. You can get them. I know you have contacts on the outside."

"What makes you say that?"

"Look, I like you, OK? I haven't shot you, have I?"

"You've shot plenty of others."

"But not you. We're like brothers, you and I. Haven't I told you my secrets?"

Lale chooses not to challenge the brotherhood claim. "You talk. I listen," says Lale.

"Sometimes you have given me advice, and I have listened. I've even tried writing nice things to my girlfriend."

"I didn't know that."

"Now you do," says Baretski, his expression earnest. "Now, listen—there's something I want you to try to get for me."

Lale is nervous that someone might overhear this conversation.

"I told you—"

"It's my girlfriend's birthday soon, and I want you to get me a pair of nylon stockings to send to her."

Lale looks at Baretski in disbelief.

Baretski smiles at him. "Just get them for me, and I won't shoot you." He laughs.

"I'll see what I can do. It might take a few days."

"Just don't take too long."

"Anything else I can do for you?" Lale asks.

"No, you've got the day off. You can go and spend time with *Gita*."

Lale cringes. It is bad enough that Baretski knows that Lale spends time with her, but how he hates hearing the bastard say her name.

Before doing what Baretski has suggested, Lale goes looking for Victor. He eventually finds Yuri, who tells him Victor is sick and not at work today. Lale says he is sorry to hear that and walks off.

"Can I do something for you?" Yuri asks.

Lale turns back. "I don't know. I have a special request."

Yuri raises an eyebrow. "I might be able to help."

"Nylon stockings. You know, the things girls wear on their legs."

"I'm not a kid, Lale. I know what nylons are."

"Could you get me a pair?" Lale reveals two diamonds in his hand.

Yuri takes them. "Give me two days. I think I can help you."

"Thanks, Yuri. Send my best to your father. I hope he's feeling better soon."

⁂

LALE IS CROSSING THE COMPOUND TO THE WOMEN'S CAMP when he hears the sound of an aircraft. He looks up as a small plane flies low over the compound and begins to circle back. So low that Lale can identify the symbol of the U.S. Air Force.

A prisoner shouts out, "It's the Americans! The Americans are here!"

Everyone looks up. A few people start jumping up and down, waving their arms in the air. Lale looks over at the towers surrounding the compound and notices the guards on full alert, training their rifles down into the compound where the men and women are making a commotion. Some of them are simply waving to get the attention of the pilot; many others are pointing toward the crematoria and screaming, "Drop the bombs. Drop the bombs!" Lale considers joining in as the plane flies over a second time and circles for a third pass. Several prisoners run toward the crematoria, pointing, desperate to get their message across. "Drop the bombs. Drop the bombs!"

On its third pass over Birkenau, the plane gains height and flies off. The prisoners continue to shout. Many drop to their knees, devastated that their cries have been ignored. Lale begins to back up against a nearby building. Just in time. Bullets rain down from the towers in the compound, hitting dozens of people too slow to move to safety.

Faced with the trigger-happy guards, Lale decides against organizing to see Gita. Instead, he goes back to his block, where he is greeted by wailing and crying. The women cradle young boys and girls who have suffered bullet wounds.

"They saw the plane and joined the other prisoners running around in the compound," says one of the men.

"What can I do to help?"

"Take the other children inside. They don't need to see this."

"Sure."

"Thanks, Lale. I'll send the old women in to help you. I don't know what to do with the bodies. I can't leave them here."

"The SS will be around to pick up the dead, I'm sure." It sounds so callous, matter-of-fact. Tears burn behind Lale's eyes. He shuffles on the spot. "I'm so sorry."

"What are they going to do with us?" the man says.

"I don't know what fate lies in store for any of us."

"To die here?"

"Not if I can help it, but I don't know."

Lale sets about gathering the young boys and girls to shepherd them indoors. Some cry; some are too shocked to cry. Several of the older women join him. They take the surviving children to the far end of the block and start telling them stories, but this time they don't work. The children cannot be comforted. Most of them remain in a silent state of trauma.

Lale goes to his room and returns with chocolate, which he and Nadya break up and offer around. Some of the children take it; others look at it as if it, too, will harm them. There is nothing more he can do. Nadya takes him by the hand, raising him to his feet.

"Thank you. You have done all you can." She brushes his cheek with the back of her hand. "Leave us now."

"I'll go and help the men," Lale responds in a faltering voice.

He staggers off outside. There, he helps the men gather the small bodies into a pile for the SS to take away. He notices that they are already picking up the bodies that lie in the compound. Several mothers refuse to hand over their precious children, and it is heartbreaking to Lale to see small, lifeless forms being wrenched from their mothers' arms.

"*Yisgadal v'yiskadash sh'mei raba*—may his name be magnified and made holy . . ." Lale recites the kaddish in a whisper. He doesn't know how or with what words the Romany honor their dead, but he feels an instinct to respond to these deaths in the way he has always known. He sits outside for a long time, looking skyward, wondering what the Americans had seen and thought. Several of the men join him in silence, a silence that is no longer quiet. A wall of grief surrounds them.

Lale thinks about the date, April 4, 1944. When he'd seen it on his work sheets that week, "April" had jarred with him. April, what was it about April? Then he realized. In three weeks' time, he will have been here for two years. *Two years.* How has he done it? How is he still breathing, when so many aren't? He thinks back to the vow he made at the beginning. To survive and to see those responsible pay. Maybe, just maybe, those in the plane had understood what was going on, and rescue was on the way. It would be too late for those who died today, but maybe their deaths would not be entirely in vain. *Hold that thought. Use it to get out of bed tomorrow morning, and the next morning, and the next.*

The twinkling of stars overhead is no longer a comfort. They merely remind him of the chasm between what life can be and what it is now. Of warm summer nights when as a boy he would sneak outside after everyone had gone to bed, to let the night breeze caress his face and lull him to sleep; of the evenings he spent with young ladies, walking hand in hand in a park, by a lake, their way lit by thousands of stars above. He always used to feel comforted by the heavenly roof of the night sky. *Somewhere, my family is looking at the same stars now and wondering where I am. I hope they can get more comfort from them than I can.*

⚬

IT WAS IN EARLY MARCH 1942 THAT LALE SAID GOODBYE TO his parents, brother, and sister in his hometown of Krompachy. He had given up his job and apartment in the city of Bratislava the previous October. He had made this decision after catching up with an old friend, a non-Jew who worked for the government. The friend had warned him that things were changing politically for all Jewish citizens and that Lale's charm would not save him from what was coming. His friend offered him a job that he said would protect him from persecution. After meeting with his friend's supervisor, Lale was offered a job as an assistant to the leader of the Slovak National Party, which he took. Dressed in a party uniform, which too closely resembled a military uniform, Lale spent several weeks traveling around the country, disseminating newsletters and speaking at rallies and gatherings. The party tried in particular to impress on youth the need to stand together, to challenge the government, which was utterly failing to denounce Hitler and offer protection to all Slovaks.

Lale knew that all Jews in Slovakia had been ordered to wear the yellow Star of David on their clothing when out in public. He had refused. Not out of fear but because he saw himself as a Slovak: proud, stubborn, and even, he conceded, arrogant about his place in the world. His being Jewish was incidental and had never before interfered with what he did or who he befriended. If it came up in conversation, he acknowledged it and moved on. It was not a defining trait for him. It was a matter discussed more often in the bedroom than in a restaurant or club.

In February 1942, he was given advance warning that the German Foreign Office had requested that the Slovak government begin transporting Jews out of the country as a source of labor. He requested leave to visit his family, which was granted, and he was told he could return to his position in the party at any time—that his job there was secure.

He never considered himself naive. Like so many living in Europe at that time, he was worried about the rise of Hitler and the horrors the Führer was inflicting on other small nations, but he couldn't accept that the Nazis would invade Slovakia. They didn't need to. The government was giving them what they wanted, when they wanted it, and posed no threat. Slovakia just wanted to be left alone. At dinners and gatherings with family and friends, they sometimes discussed the reports of persecution of Jews in other countries, but they did not consider that Slovak Jews as a group were particularly at risk.

❧

AND YET HERE HE IS NOW. TWO YEARS HAVE PASSED. HE LIVES in a community largely split into two—Jewish and Romany—identified by their race, not their nationality, and this is something Lale still cannot understand. Nations can threaten other nations. They have power, they have militaries. *How can a race that is spread out across multiple countries be considered a threat?* For as long as he lives, be it short or long, he knows he will never comprehend this.

19

Have you lost your faith?" Gita asks as she leans back into Lale's chest at their place behind the administration building. She has chosen this moment to ask the question because she wants to hear his response, not see it.

"Why do you ask?" he says, stroking the back of her head.

"Because I think you have," she says, "and that saddens me."

"Then clearly you haven't lost yours?"

"I asked first."

"Yes, I think I have," Lale answers.

"When?"

"The first night I arrived here. I told you what happened, what I saw. How any merciful god could let that happen, I don't know. And nothing has happened since that night to change my mind. Quite the opposite."

"You have to believe in something."

"I do. I believe in you and me, and getting out of here, and making a life together where we can—"

"I know, whenever and wherever we want." She sighs. "Oh, Lale, if only."

Lale turns her around to face him.

"I will not be defined by being a Jew," he says. "I won't deny it, but I am a man first, a man in love with you."

"And if I want to keep my faith? If it is still important to me?"

"I have no say in that."

"Yes, you do."

They fall into an uneasy silence. He watches her, her eyes downcast.

"I have no problem with you keeping your faith," says Lale gently. "In fact, I will encourage your faith if it means a lot to you and keeps you by my side. When we leave here, I will encourage you to practice your faith, and when our babies come along, they can follow their mother's faith. Does that satisfy you?"

"Babies? I don't know if I will be able to have children. I think I'm screwed up inside."

"Once we leave here and I can fatten you up a little, we will have babies, and they will be beautiful babies; they will take after their mother."

"Thank you, my love. You make me want to believe in a future."

"Good. Does that mean you will tell me your last name and where you come from?"

"Not yet. I told you, on the day we leave this place. Please don't ask me again."

AFTER PARTING FROM GITA, LALE SEEKS OUT LEON AND A FEW others from Block 7. It's a beautiful summer's day, and he intends to enjoy the sun and his friends while he can. They sit against the wall of one of the blocks. Their conversation is simple. At the sound of the siren, Lale says his goodbyes and makes his way back to his block. As he nears the building, he senses that something is wrong. The Romany children stand around, not running to meet him but stepping aside as he walks by. He greets them, but they don't respond. He understands why immediately when he opens the door to his room. Displayed on his bed are the gems and currency from under his mattress. Two SS officers are waiting.

"Care to explain this, Tätowierer?"

Lale can find no words.

One of the officers snatches his bag from his hands and empties his tools and ink bottles onto the floor. Then they put the bounty into the bag. With pistols drawn, they face Lale squarely and motion for him to move. The children stand aside as Lale is marched out of the camp for what he believes will be the last time.

⁓

LALE STANDS IN FRONT OF HOUSTEK, THE CONTENTS OF HIS bag spread out over the Oberscharführer's desk.

Houstek picks up and examines each precious stone and piece of jewelry, one at a time. "Where did you get all this?" he asks, not looking up.

"Prisoners gave it to me."

"Which prisoners?"

"I do not know their names."

Houstek looks up at Lale sharply. "You don't know who gave you all this?"

"No, I do not."

"I'm meant to believe that?"

"Yes, sir. They bring it to me, but I do not ask them their names."

Houstek slams his fist on the desk, causing the gems to jangle.

"This makes me very angry, Tätowierer. You are good at your job. Now I will have to find someone else to do it." He turns to the escorting officers. "Take him to Block 11. He'll soon remember the names there."

Lale is marched out and placed in a truck. Two SS officers sit on either side of him, each ramming a pistol into his ribs. During the two-and-a-half-mile drive Lale silently says goodbye to Gita and the future they were just imagining. Closing his eyes, he mentally says the names of each of his family members. He cannot picture his siblings as clearly as he used to. His mother he can see perfectly. But how do you say goodbye to your mother? The person who gave you breath, who taught you how to live? He cannot say goodbye to her. He gasps as his father's image comes before him, causing one of the officers to push his pistol harder into his ribs. The last time he saw his father, he was crying. He doesn't want this to be how he remembers him, so he searches for another image and comes up with his father working with his beloved horses. He always spoke so warmly to them, in contrast to the way he expressed himself to his children. Lale's brother, Max, older and wiser. He tells him he hopes he hasn't let him down, that he has tried to act as Max would have in his place. When he thinks of his little sister, Goldie, the pain is too much.

The truck comes to a sudden halt, throwing Lale against the officer next to him.

He is placed in a small room in Block 11. The reputation of Blocks 10 and 11 is well-known. They are the punishment blocks. Behind these secluded torture houses stands the Black Wall, the execution wall. Lale expects that he will be taken there after being tortured.

For two days he sits in the cell, the only light coming in through a crack under the door. While he listens to the cries and screams of others, he relives every moment he has spent with Gita.

On the third day, he is blinded by sunlight spilling into the room. A large man blocks the doorway and hands him a bowl of liquid. Lale takes it, and as his eyes adjust, he recognizes the man.

"Jakub, is that you?"

Jakub enters the room, the low ceiling forcing him to stoop.

"Tätowierer. What are you doing here?" Jakub is visibly shocked.

Lale struggles to his feet, his hand outstretched. "I often wondered what had happened to you," he says.

"As you predicted, they found work for me."

"So you're a guard?"

"Not just a guard, my friend." Jakub's voice is grim. "Sit and eat, and I will tell you what I do here and what will happen to you."

Apprehensively, Lale sits and looks at the food Jakub has given him. A thin, dirty broth containing a single piece of potato. Starving a few moments ago, he finds that his appetite has now left him.

"I have never forgotten your kindness," Jakub says. "I was sure I would die of starvation the night I arrived here, and there you were to feed me."

"Well, you need more food than most."

"I've heard stories of you smuggling food. Are they true?"

"That's why I'm in here. The prisoners working in the Canada smuggle me money and gems, and I use them to buy food and medicine from the villagers, which I distribute. I guess someone missed out and told on me."

"You don't know who?"

"Do you?"

"No, it's not my job to know. My job is to get names from you—names of prisoners who might be planning to escape or resist, and, of course, the names of the prisoners who get the money and jewels to you."

Lale looks away. The enormity of what Jakub is saying begins to register.

"Like you, Tätowierer, I do what I have to do to survive."

Lale nods.

"I am to beat you until you give me names. I am a killer, Lale."

Lale shakes his hanging head, mutters every swear word he knows.

"I have no choice."

Mixed emotions race through Lale. Names of dead prisoners flit through his mind. Could he give Jakub those names? *No. They'll find out eventually, and then I'll be back here again.*

"The thing is," Jakub says, "I can't let you give me any names."

Lale stares, confused.

"You were kind to me and I will make the beating look worse than it is, but I will kill you before I let you tell me a name. I want as little innocent blood on my hands as possible," Jakub explains.

"Oh, Jakub. I never imagined this would be the work they found for you. I'm so sorry."

"If I must kill one Jew to save ten others, then I will."

Lale reaches his hand up to the large man's shoulder. "Do what you have to."

"Speak only in Yiddish," says Jakub, turning away. "I don't think the SS here know you, or that you speak German."

"OK, Yiddish it is."

"I'll come back later."

Back in darkness, Lale ponders his fate. He resolves to speak no names. It is now a matter of who kills him: a bored SS officer whose supper is getting cold, or Jakub, carrying out a just killing to save others. A sense of calm comes over him as he resigns himself to death.

Will someone tell Gita what happened to him, he wonders, or will she spend the rest of her life never knowing?

Lale falls into a deep, exhausted sleep.

⁓

"WHERE IS HE?" HIS FATHER ROARS, STORMING INTO THE house.

Once again, Lale has not turned up to work. His father is late coming home for supper because he had to do Lale's work for him. Lale runs and tries to hide behind his mother, pulling her away from the bench where she stands, putting a barrier between himself and his father. She reaches behind herself and grabs hold of whatever part of Lale or his clothing she can, protecting him from what would otherwise be a cuff over the head at the very least. His father doesn't force her away or make any further attempt to reach Lale.

"I'll deal with him," his mother says. "After dinner I'll punish him. Now sit down."

Lale's brother and sister roll their eyes. They've seen and heard it all before.

Later that evening, Lale promises his mother he will try to be more helpful to his father. But it is so hard to help his father out. Lale fears he will end up like him, old before his time, too tired to pay his wife a simple compliment about her looks or the food she spends all day preparing for him. That is not who Lale wants to be.

"I'm your favorite, aren't I, Mama?" Lale would ask. If the two of them were alone in the house, his mother would hug him tightly. "Yes, my darling, you are." If his brother or sister were present, "You are all my favorites." Lale never heard his brother or sister ask this question, but they might have in his absence. When he was a young boy, he would often announce to his family that he was going to marry his mother when he grew up. His father would pretend not to hear. His siblings would goad Lale into a fight, pointing out that their mother was already married. After breaking up their fights, his mother would take him aside and explain to him that he would find someone else one day to love and care for. He never wanted to believe her.

As he became a young man he would run home to his mother each day for the hugged greeting, the feel of her comforting body, her soft skin, the kisses she planted on his forehead.

"What can I do to help you?" he would say.

"You're such a good boy. You will make someone a wonderful husband one day."

"Tell me what to do to be a good husband. I don't want to be like Papa. He doesn't make you smile. He doesn't help you."

"Your papa works very hard to earn money for us to live."

"I know, but can't he do both? Earn money and make you smile?"

"You have a lot to learn before you grow up, young man."

"Then teach me. I want the girl I marry to like me, to be happy with me."

Lale's mother sat down, and he took a seat across from her. "You must first learn to listen to her. Even if you are tired, never be too tired to listen to what she has to say. Learn what she likes and, more important, what she doesn't like. When you can, give her little treats—flowers, chocolates. Women like those things."

"When was the last time Papa brought you a treat?"

"It doesn't matter. You want to know what girls want, not what I get."

"When I've got money, I'll bring you flowers and chocolates, I promise."

"You should save your money for the girl who captures your heart."

"How will I know who she is?"

"Oh, you'll know."

She drew him into her arms and stroked his hair: her boy, her young man.

⁓

HER IMAGE DISSOLVES—TEARS, THE PICTURE BLURS, HE blinks—and he imagines Gita in his arms, him stroking her hair.

"You were right, Mama. I do know."

⁓

JAKUB COMES FOR HIM. HE DRAGS HIM DOWN A CORRIDOR TO A small, windowless room. A single light bulb hangs from the ceiling. Handcuffs dangle from a chain on the back wall. There is a birch rod lying on the floor. Two SS officers talk together, seemingly oblivious to Lale's presence. He shuffles backward, not raising his eyes above the floor. Without warning, Jakub swings a punch into Lale's face, sending him stumbling back against the wall. The officers now pay attention. Lale attempts to stand. Jakub winds his right foot slowly back. Lale anticipates the coming kick. He backs away just as Jakub's foot connects with his ribs, then exaggerates the impact by rolling and heaving and clutching his chest. As he slowly rises, Jakub punches him in the face again. He takes the full force this time, though Jakub had telegraphed his intention to hit him. Blood runs freely from his smashed nose. Jakub pulls Lale roughly to his feet and handcuffs him to the dangling chain.

Jakub picks up the birch, tears the shirt from Lale's back, and lashes him five times. Then he pulls Lale's trousers and underpants down and whips him across the buttocks five more times. Lale's yelps are not feigned. Jakub jerks Lale's head back.

"Give us the names of the prisoners who steal for you!" Jakub says, firm and menacing.

The officers look on, standing casually.

Lale shakes his head, whimpering, "I don't know." Jakub strikes Lale ten more times. Blood runs down his legs. The two officers begin to pay more attention and step closer. Jakub jerks Lale's head back and snarls at him, "Talk!" He whispers in his ear, "Say you don't know and then faint." And then louder, "Give us the names!"

"I never ask! I don't know. You have to believe me—"

Jakub punches Lale in the stomach. He buckles at the knees, rolls his eyes back, and pretends to pass out. Jakub turns to the SS officers.

"He is a weak Jew. If he knew the names, he would've told us by now." He kicks Lale's legs as he dangles from the chain.

The officers nod and walk from the room.

The door closes and Jakub quickly releases Lale, laying him gently on the floor. With a cloth hidden in his shirt, he wipes the blood from Lale's body and gently pulls up his pants for him.

"I'm so sorry, Lale."

He helps him to his feet, carries him back to his room, and lays him on his stomach.

"You did good. You'll need to sleep like this for a while. I'll come back later with some water and a clean shirt. Get some rest now."

⤙⤚

OVER THE NEXT FEW DAYS, JAKUB VISITS LALE EACH DAY WITH food, water, and the occasional change of shirt. He reports to Lale the extent of his injuries and that they are healing. Lale knows he will be marked for life. *Perhaps the Tätowierer deserves that.*

"How many times did you strike me?" Lale asks.

"I don't know."

"Yes, you do."

"It's over, Lale, and you're healing. Leave it alone."

"Did you break my nose? I'm having trouble breathing through it."

"Probably, but not too bad. The swelling's gone down, and it's hardly out of shape. You're still handsome. You'll still have the girls chasing you."

"I don't want girls chasing me."

"Why not?"

"I've found the one I want."

The next day the door opens and Lale looks up to greet Jakub, but instead there are two SS officers. They indicate that Lale should get to his feet and come with them. Lale stays sitting as he tries to compose himself. *Can this be the end? I am for the Black Wall?* He silently says his goodbyes to his family and, last, to Gita. The SS become impatient, step into his room, and point their rifles at him. He follows them outside on trembling legs. Feeling the sun on his face for the first time in more than a week, he staggers along between the two officers. Looking up, preparing to meet his fate, he sees several other prisoners being bundled into a nearby truck. *Maybe this isn't the end.* His legs give out, and the officers drag him the remaining short distance. They throw him on and he doesn't look back. He clings to the side of the truck all the way to Birkenau.

20

LALE IS HELPED FROM THE TRUCK AND DRAGGED BACK INTO Houstek's office. The two SS officers each hold one of his arms.

"We got nothing out of him, even after the big Jew had a go," one of them says.

Houstek turns to Lale, who raises his head.

"So you really didn't know their names? And the officers didn't shoot you?"

"No, sir."

"And now they've returned you to me. Now you're my problem again."

"Yes, sir."

Houstek addresses the officers.

"Take him to Block 31." He turns to Lale. "We will get some hard work out of you before your number is up, mark my words."

Lale is dragged from the office. He tries to keep pace with the SS officers, but halfway across the compound he gives up and sacrifices the skin on the tops of his feet to the gravel. The officers open the door to Block 31 and toss him inside before taking their leave. Lale lies on the floor, exhausted in body and soul. Several inmates approach him cautiously. Two try to help him up, but Lale cries out in pain and they stop. One of the men pulls up Lale's shirt, revealing the large welts across his back and buttocks. More gently this time, they pick him up and place him on a bunk. He soon falls asleep.

⤳

"I KNOW WHO THIS IS," ONE OF THE PRISONERS SAYS.

"Who?" another asks.

"It's the Tätowierer. Don't you recognize him? He probably made your number."

"Yeah, you're right. I wonder who he pissed off."

"I got extra rations from him when I was in Block 6. He was always handing out food."

"I've never heard about that. I've only been in this block. I pissed someone off the day I arrived." The men chuckle quietly.

"He can't make it to supper. I'll bring him some of mine. He's gonna need it tomorrow."

A short while later Lale is woken by two men, each with a small piece of bread. They offer them to him, and he gratefully accepts.

"I've got to get out of here."

The men laugh.

"Sure, my friend. You have two options, then: one is quick, the other might take a little longer."

"And what are they?"

"Well, tomorrow morning you can go outside and throw yourself on the death cart when it comes around. Or you can come and work in the fields with us until you drop or beg them to shoot you."

"I don't like those options. I'll have to find another way."

"Good luck, my friend. You'd better get some rest. You've got a long day ahead of you, especially in your condition."

⁂

THAT NIGHT, LALE DREAMS OF HIS DEPARTURES FROM HOME.

The first time he'd left home, he was a young man full of promise, in search of a future to make his own. He would find a job he enjoyed and could grow in. He would have rich experiences, visiting the romantic cities of Europe that he'd read about: Paris, Rome, Vienna. Above all, he wanted to find that one person he would fall in love with, shower with affection and the things his mother had said were important: flowers, chocolates, his time and attention.

His second departure, full of uncertainty and the unknown, had rattled him. What lay ahead?

He arrived in Prague after a long, emotionally painful journey away from his family. He reported as instructed to the relevant government department and was told to find accommodations nearby and to report back weekly until his role was decided. On April 16, a month later, he was told to report with his belongings to a local school. There, he was housed with a number of young Jewish men from across Slovakia.

Lale prided himself on his appearance, and his living situation did not prevent him from looking his best. Each day, he washed and cleaned his clothes in the school bathroom. He didn't know where he was headed, but he wanted to make damned sure he looked his best when he arrived.

After five days of sitting around, bored, frightened—mostly bored—Lale and the others were told to gather up their possessions and were marched to the railway station. They were told nothing about where they were going. A train designed to transport cattle pulled up, and the men were ordered to climb aboard. Some objected, explaining that the filthy wagon insulted their dignity. Lale watched the response, seeing for the first time his fellow countrymen raising their rifles at Jews and striking the ones who continued protesting. He climbed on board along with all the others. When no one else could be pushed into his wagon, Lale watched as the doors were slammed shut and heard them bolted by members of the Slovak army, men whose job it should have been to protect him.

Over and over he hears the sound of the doors being slammed and bolted, slammed and bolted.

⸺

THE NEXT MORNING, THE TWO KIND PRISONERS HELP LALE from the block and stand with him to await roll call. *How long has it been since I've stood like this?* Numbers, numbers. Survival is always about your number. Being ticked off your kapo's list tells you that you are still alive. Lale's number is last on the list, since he is the newest occupant of Block 31. He doesn't respond the first time it is called, has to be nudged. After a cup of old, weak coffee and a thin slice of stale bread, they are marched off toward their labor.

In a field between the two camps of Auschwitz and Birkenau, they are made to carry large rocks from one side to the other. When the rocks have all been moved over, they are told to take them back again. And so the day goes on. Lale thinks of the hundreds of times he has walked the road alongside and seen this activity taking place. *No, I only glimpsed it. I couldn't watch what these men were enduring.* He quickly works out that the SS shoot the last one to arrive with his rock.

Lale needs to use all of his strength. His muscles ache, but his mind stays strong. On one occasion he is the second to last to arrive. When the day ends, those still living gather up the bodies of those slain and carry them back to the camp. Lale is excused from this task, but is told he has one day's grace only. Tomorrow he will have to pull his weight, provided he's still alive.

As they trudge back into Birkenau, Lale sees Baretski standing inside the gates. He falls into step beside Lale.

"I heard what happened to you."

Lale looks at him. "Baretski, can you help me with something?" By asking for assistance, he is admitting to the other men that he is different from them. He knows the officer's name and can ask him for help. Marking himself as friendly with the enemy brings acute shame, but he needs this.

"Maybe . . . What is it?" Baretski looks uncomfortable.

"Can you get a message to Gita?"

"Do you really want her to know where you are? Isn't it better that she thinks you're already dead?"

"Just tell her exactly where I am—Block 31—and tell her to tell Cilka."

"You want her friend to know where you are?"

"Yes, it's important. She'll understand."

"Hmm. I'll do it if I feel like it. Is it true you had a fortune in diamonds under your mattress?"

"Did they mention the rubies and emeralds, the Yankee dollars, the British and South African pounds?"

Baretski shakes his head, laughing, slapping Lale painfully on the back as he walks off.

"Cilka. Gita must tell Cilka," he calls after him.

A backward wave of Baretski's arm dismisses Lale.

~

BARETSKI ENTERS THE WOMEN'S CAMP AS THEY ARE LINING UP
for dinner. Cilka sees him approach the kapo and then point at
Gita. The kapo beckons Gita with her finger. Cilka draws Dana in
close as Gita slowly walks over to Baretski. They cannot hear what
he says, but his message causes Gita to cover her face with her hands.
She then turns toward her friends and runs back into their arms.

"He's alive! Lale is alive," she says. "He said I'm to tell you,
Cilka, that he is in Block 31."

"Why me?"

"I don't know, but he said Lale insisted I tell you."

"What can *she* do?" Dana asks.

Cilka looks away, her mind working feverishly.

"I don't know," says Gita, not in the mood to analyze. "I only
know that he is alive."

"Cilka, what can you do? How can you help?" Dana pleads.

"I will think about it," says Cilka.

"He's alive. My love is alive," Gita repeats.

~

THAT NIGHT, CILKA LIES IN SCHWARZHUBER'S ARMS. SHE CAN
tell he is not yet asleep. She opens her mouth to say something
but is silenced by him retrieving his arm from underneath her.

"Are you all right?" she asks tentatively, fearing he will be suspicious of such an intimate question.

"Yes."

There is a softness in his voice she has not heard before, and, emboldened, Cilka presses on. "I have never said no to anything for you, have I? And I've never asked you for anything before?" she says tentatively.

"That's true," he responds.

"Can I ask for one thing?"

⁓

LALE MAKES IT THROUGH THE NEXT DAY. HE DOES HIS BIT, helping to carry one of the murdered men back. He hates himself for having thoughts only of the pain it causes him, with little compassion for the dead man. *What is happening to me?* Step by step, the pain in his shoulders threatens to drag him down. *Fight it, fight it.*

As they enter the camp, Lale's attention is caught by two people standing just beyond the fence that separates the prisoners' blocks from the staff quarters. The diminutive Cilka stands beside Schwarzhuber. A guard on Lale's side of the fence is talking to them. Lale stops, slackening his grip on the corpse, which causes the prisoner at the other end of the body to stumble and fall. Lale looks at Cilka, who peers back at him before saying something to Schwarzhuber. He nods and points to Lale. Cilka and Schwarzhuber walk away as the guard approaches Lale.

"Come with me."

Lale rests the legs he's been carrying on the ground and looks for the first time at the dead man's face. His compassion returns, and he bows his head at this tragic end to yet another life. He gives an apologetic glance to the other man carrying the body and hurries to follow the guard. The other inmates of Block 31 all stare after him.

The guard tells Lale, "I'm instructed to take you to your old room in the Gypsy camp."

"I know the way."

"Suit yourself." The guard leaves him.

Lale stops outside the Romany camp, watching the children run around. Several of them look at him, trying to make sense of his return. The Tätowierer, they have been told, is dead. One of them runs to Lale and throws his arms around his waist, hugging him tight, welcoming him "home." The others join in, and before long adults are coming out of the block to greet him. "Where have you been?" they ask. "Are you injured?" He deflects all their questions.

Nadya is standing at the back of the group. Lale makes eye contact with her. Pushing his way through the men, women, and children, he stops in front of her. With a finger, he wipes a tear from her cheek. "It's good to see you, Nadya."

"We've missed you. I've missed you."

All Lale can do is nod. He needs to get away quickly before he breaks down in front of everyone. He rushes to his room, closes the door on the world, and lies on his old bed.

21

A RE YOU SURE YOU'RE NOT A CAT?"
Lale hears the words and struggles to register where he is.
He opens his eyes to find a grinning Baretski leaning over him.

"What?"

"You must be a cat, because you sure have more lives than anyone else here."

Lale struggles to sit up.

"It was—"

"Cilka, yes, I know. Must be nice to have friends in high places."

"I'd gladly give my life for her not to need such friends."

"You nearly did give your life. Not that it would've helped
her."

"Yeah, that's one situation I can't do anything about."

Baretski laughs. "You really think you run these camps, don't
you? Hell, maybe you do. You're still alive, and you shouldn't be.
How did you get out of Block 11?"

"I have no idea. When they took me out, I was sure I was headed for the Black Wall, but then I was thrown in a truck and brought back here."

"I've never known anyone to walk away from the Strafkompanie—so well done," Baretski says.

"That's one piece of history I don't mind making. How come I've got my old room back?"

"Easy. It comes with the job."

"What?"

"You're the Tätowierer, and all I can say is, thank god. The eunuch who replaced you was no match."

"Houstek is letting me have my job back?"

"I wouldn't go anywhere near him. He didn't want you back; he wanted you shot. It was Schwarzhuber who had other plans for you."

"I need to get my hands on at least some chocolate for Cilka."

"Tätowierer, don't. You will be watched very closely. Now come on, I'll take you to work."

As they are leaving the room, Lale says, "I'm sorry I wasn't able to get you the nylons you wanted. I'd made arrangements but got derailed."

"Mm, well, at least you tried. Anyway, she's not my girlfriend anymore. She dumped me."

"Sorry to hear that. I hope it wasn't because of something I suggested you say to her."

"I don't think so. She just met someone who is in the same town—hell, the same country—as her."

Lale considers saying something more but decides to let it drop. Baretski leads him out of his block and into the compound, where a truckload of men has arrived and a selection is taking place. He smiles inwardly at the sight of Leon working, dropping the tattoo stick, spilling ink. Baretski wanders off, and Lale approaches Leon from behind.

"Need a hand?"

Leon turns around, knocking a bottle of ink over as he grasps Lale by the hand, shaking it vigorously, overjoyed.

"It's so good to see you!" he cries.

"Believe me, it's good to be back. How are you?"

"Still pissing sitting down. Otherwise, I'm OK. So much better now that you're here."

"Let's get on with it, then. Looks like they're sending quite a few our way."

"Does Gita know you're back?" Leon asks.

"I think so. It was her friend Cilka who got me out."

"The one who . . . ?"

"Yes. I'll try to see them tomorrow. Give me one of those sticks. I'd better not give them any excuse to throw me back where I was."

Leon holds out his tattoo stick as he rummages around in Lale's bag for another one. Together they begin work, tattooing the newest residents of Birkenau.

❧

THE NEXT AFTERNOON, LALE WAITS OUTSIDE THE ADMINIStration building as the girls leave work. Dana and Gita don't see him until he is standing right in front of them, blocking their path. A moment passes before they react. Then both girls throw their arms around him and hug him tightly. Dana cries. No tears come from Gita. Lale releases them and takes each by the hand.

"Both still beautiful," he tells them.

Gita smacks him on the arm with her free hand.

"I thought you were dead. Again. I thought I'd never see you again."

"Me, too," says Dana.

"But I'm not. Thanks to you, and to Cilka, I'm not. I'm here with the two of you, where I should be."

"But . . ." cries Gita.

Lale pulls her toward him and holds her securely.

Dana kisses him on the cheek. "I'll leave you two. It's so good to see you, Lale. I thought Gita would die of a broken heart if you didn't come back soon."

"Thank you, Dana," says Lale. "You're a good friend, to both of us."

She walks off, the smile not leaving her face.

Hundreds of prisoners mill around the compound as they stand there, not knowing what to do next.

"Close your eyes," Lale says.

"What?"

"Close them and count to ten."

"But—"

"Just do it."

One eye at a time, Gita does as she is told. She counts to ten, then opens them. "I don't understand."

"I'm still here. I'll never leave you again."

"Come on, we have to keep moving," she tells him.

They walk toward the women's camp. With no bribe for the kapo, Lale can't risk Gita getting back late. They gently lean in toward each other.

"I don't know how much longer I can stand this."

"It can't last forever, my darling. Just hang in there, please hang in there. We'll have the rest of our lives together."

"But—"

"No buts. I promised you we'd leave this place and make a life together."

"How can we? We can't even know what tomorrow will bring. Look at what just happened to you."

"I'm here with you now, aren't I?"

"Lale—"

"Leave it, Gita."

"Will you tell me what happened to you? Where you've been?"

Lale shakes his head. "No. I'm back here with you now. What matters is what I've told you many times, that we will leave this place and have a free life together. Trust me, Gita."

"I do."

Lale likes the sound of that.

"One day you will say those two little words to me under different circumstances. In front of a rabbi, surrounded by our family and friends."

Gita giggles and lays her head briefly on his shoulder as they reach the entrance to the women's camp.

⁓

As Lale walks back to his block, two youths approach and walk alongside him.

"You're the Tätowierer?"

"Who's asking?" says Lale.

"We hear you might be able to get us some extra food."

"Whoever told you that was mistaken."

"We can pay," one of them says, opening his clenched fist to reveal a small but perfect diamond.

Lale grits his teeth.

"Go on, take it. If you can get us anything, we would really appreciate it, mister."

"What block are you in?"

"Nine."

How many lives does a cat have?

⇌

THE NEXT MORNING, LALE HANGS AROUND THE MAIN GATES, bag in hand. Twice, SS approach him.

"Politische Abteilung," he says on both occasions, and is left alone. But he is more apprehensive than he used to be. Victor and Yuri break from the line of men entering the camp and greet Lale warmly.

"Can we ask where you've been?" Victor asks.

"Best not," Lale replies.

"You back in business?"

"Not like before. I'm scaling it down, OK? Just a little extra food, if you can. No more nylons."

"Sure. Welcome back," Victor says with enthusiasm.

Lale extends his hand, Victor takes it, and the diamond changes hands.

"Down payment. See you tomorrow?"

"Tomorrow."

Yuri looks on. "It's good to see you again," he says quietly.

"You too, Yuri. Have you grown?"

"Yeah, I reckon I have."

"Say," says Lale, "you wouldn't happen to have any chocolate on you? I really need to spend some time with my girl."

Yuri takes a block out of his bag and hands it to Lale with a wink.

Lale heads straight to the women's camp and Block 29. The kapo is where she always is, soaking up the sun. She watches Lale approach.

"Tätowierer, good to see you again," she says.

"Have you lost weight? You're looking good," Lale says with the merest hint of irony.

"You haven't been around for a while."

"I'm back now." He hands her the chocolate.

"I'll get her for you."

He watches her walk toward the administration building and speak to a female SS officer outside. Then he enters the block and sits, waiting for Gita to walk through the door. He doesn't have to wait long before she appears. She closes the door and walks toward him. He stands and leans on the bunk post. He fears he will struggle to say the words he needs to. He arranges his face into a mask of self-control.

"To make love whenever and wherever we want. We may not be free, but I choose now and I choose here. What do you say?"

She throws herself into his arms, smothering his face with kisses. As they begin to undress, Lale stops and holds Gita's hands.

"You asked me if I would tell you where I disappeared to, and I said no, remember?"

"Yes."

"Well, I still don't want to talk about it, but there is something I can't keep from you. Now, you're not to be frightened, and I'm all right, but I did take a little bit of a beating."

"Show me."

Lale slides his shirt off slowly and turns his back to her. She says nothing but runs her fingers ever so softly over the welts on his back. Her lips follow, and he knows that nothing more needs to be said. Their lovemaking is slow and gentle. He feels tears well up and fights them back. This is the deepest love he's ever felt.

22

LALE SPENDS LONG, HOT SUMMER DAYS WITH GITA, OR WITH thoughts of her. His workload hasn't diminished, though; quite the opposite: thousands of Hungarian Jews are now arriving in Auschwitz and Birkenau every week. As a result, unrest breaks out in both the men's and women's camps. Lale has worked out why. The higher the number on a person's arm, the less respect they receive from everyone else. Every time another nationality arrives in large numbers, turf wars ensue. Gita has told him about the women's camp. The Slovak girls, who have been in there longest, resent the Hungarian girls, who refuse to accept that they aren't entitled to the same small perks the Slovaks have worked hard to negotiate. She and her friends feel that surviving what they have should count for something. They have, for example, obtained casual clothing from the Canada. No more blue-and-white-striped pajamas for them. And they are not prepared to share. The SS do not take sides when fights break out; all involved are punished with an equal lack of mercy. They are denied their meager food rations; they might be flogged: sometimes it's just the one blow with a rifle butt or swagger stick, but at other times they are beaten savagely while their fellow prisoners are forced to look on.

Gita and Dana keep clear of any fights. Gita has enough issues dealing with petty jealousies over her job in the administration building, her friendship with the seemingly protected Cilka, and, of course, visits from her boyfriend, the Tätowierer.

Lale is largely immune to the camp disputes. Working with Leon and only a handful of other prisoners alongside the SS, he is removed from the plight of the thousands of starving men who must work and fight and live and die together. Living among the Romany also gives him a sense of security and belonging. He realizes he has settled into a pattern of life that is comfortable relative to the conditions of the majority. He works when he has to, spends whatever time he can steal with Gita, plays with the Romany children, and talks to their parents—mostly the younger men, but also the older women. He loves how they care for everyone, not only their biological family. He doesn't connect so well with the older men, who mostly sit around not engaging with the children, the young adults, or even the older women. When he looks at them, he often thinks about his own father.

LATE ONE NIGHT LALE IS WOKEN BY YELLING SS, BARKING dogs, and screaming women and children. He opens his door and looks out to see the men, women, and children in his block being forced from the building. He watches until the last woman, clutching an infant, is shoved brutally out into the night. He follows them all outside and stands, stunned, as all around him the other

Romany blocks are also emptied. Thousands of people are being herded onto nearby trucks. The compound is lit up, and dozens of SS and their dogs corral the mob, shooting at anyone who doesn't respond immediately to the instruction, "Get on the truck!"

Lale stops a passing officer he recognizes. "Where are you taking them?" he asks.

"You want to join them, Tätowierer?" the man responds, walking on.

Lale sinks into the shadows, scanning the crowd. He sees Nadya and runs to her. "Nadya," he pleads. "Don't go."

She forces a brave smile. "I don't have a choice, Lale. I go where my people go. Goodbye, my friend, it's been . . ." An officer pushes her along before she can finish.

Lale stands paralyzed, watching until the last person has been loaded onto the trucks. The trucks drive off, and slowly he walks back into the eerily silent block. He goes back to bed. Sleep will not come.

IN THE MORNING LALE, DISTRAUGHT, JOINS LEON, AND THEY work furiously as new transports arrive.

Mengele is scanning the silent rows, making his way slowly toward the tattooists' station. Leon's hands tremble at his approach. Lale tries to give him a reassuring look. But the bastard who has mutilated him is only a few feet away. Mengele stops and watches them work. Occasionally he peers closely at a tattoo, increasing Lale's and Leon's agitation. His deathly smirk never leaves his face. He attempts eye contact with Lale, who never raises his eyes above the level of the arm he is working on.

"Tätowierer, Tätowierer," Mengele says, leaning over the table, "maybe today I will take you." He tilts his head, seeming to enjoy Lale's discomfort. Then, having had his fun, he ambles away.

Something light lands on Lale's head and he looks up. Ash is belching from the nearby crematorium. He starts to tremble and drops his tattoo stick. Leon tries to steady him.

"Lale, what is it? What's wrong?"

Lale's scream is choked by a sob. "You bastards, you fucking bastards!"

Leon grips Lale's arm, trying to get him to control himself as Mengele looks their way and starts to walk back over. Lale is seeing red. He is out of control. *Nadya*. He tries desperately to rein himself in as Mengele arrives. He feels as though he might vomit.

Mengele's breath is in his face. "Is everything all right here?"

"Yes, Herr Doktor, everything is fine," Leon answers shakily.

Leon bends down and picks up Lale's stick.

"Just a broken stick. We'll fix it and be right back to work," Leon continues.

"You don't look well, Tätowierer. Would you like me to take a look at you?" Mengele asks.

"I'm fine, just a broken stick," Lale coughs. He keeps his head down, turns away, and tries to get back to work.

"Tätowierer!" Mengele barks.

Lale turns back toward Mengele, jaw clenched, head still low. Mengele has unholstered his pistol. He holds it limply at his side.

"I could have you shot for turning away from me." He raises the weapon, pointing it at Lale's forehead. "Look at me. I could shoot you right now. What do you say to that?"

Lale raises his head but moves his gaze to the doctor's forehead, refusing to look into his eyes. "Yes, Herr Doktor. I'm sorry, it won't happen again, Herr Doktor," he mutters.

"Get back to work. You're holding things up," Mengele barks, and again walks off. Lale looks at Leon and points to the ash now falling all around them.

"They emptied the Gypsy camp last night."

Leon hands Lale his tattoo stick before going back to work himself, in silence. Lale looks up, searching for the sun to shine down on him. But it is concealed by ash and smoke.

That evening he returns to his block, which is now occupied by people that he and Leon marked earlier. He shuts himself away in his room. He doesn't want to make friends. Not tonight. Not ever. He wants only silence in his block.

23

FOR WEEKS, LALE AND GITA'S TIME TOGETHER IS SPENT mostly in silence as she tries in vain to console him. He has told her what happened, and while she understands his distress, she doesn't share it to the same degree. It isn't her fault she never got to know Lale's "other family." She had delighted in hearing his stories of the children and their attempts to play, with no toys, kicking balls made out of snow or debris, seeing who could jump the highest to touch the timber slats on their building, mostly just playing tag. She tries to get him to talk about his biological family, but Lale has become stubborn and is refusing to say anything more until she shares information about her own life. Gita doesn't know how to break the spell of Lale's grief. They have both withstood, for more than two and a half years, the worst of humanity. But this is the first time she's seen Lale sink to this depth of depression. "What about the thousands of our people?" she yells at him one day. "What about what you have seen at Auschwitz, with

Mengele? Do you know how many people have been through these two camps? *Do you?*" Lale does not reply. "I see the cards with the names and ages—babies, grandparents—I see their names and their numbers. I can't even count that high."

Lale doesn't need Gita to remind him of the number of people who have passed through the camps. He has marked their skin himself. He looks at her; she is studying the ground. He realizes that while to him they were just numbers, to Gita they were names. Her job means that she knows more about these people than he does. She knows their names and ages, and he realizes that this knowledge will forever haunt her.

"I'm sorry, you're right," he says. "Any death is one too many. I'll try not to be so gloomy."

"I want you to be yourself with me, but it's been going on for too long, Lale, and one day is a long time for us."

"Smart, and beautiful. I'll never forget them, you know?"

"I couldn't love you if you did. They were your family, I know that. I know it's a strange thing for me to say, but you will honor them by staying alive, surviving this place and telling the world what happened here."

Lale leans over to kiss her, his heart weighted by love and sorrow.

A massive explosion rings out, shaking the ground beneath them. From their spot behind the administration block they jump to their feet and run to the front of the building. A second explosion makes them look toward the nearby crematorium, where smoke is rising and pandemonium is breaking out. The prison workers are running from the building, most of them toward the fence that surrounds the camp. Gunfire erupts from the top of the crematorium. Lale looks up and sees Sonderkommando up there, shooting wildly. The SS fire heavy machine guns in retaliation. Within minutes, they have put an end to the shooting.

"What's happening?" Gita says.

"I don't know. We need to get indoors."

Bullets strike the ground around them as the SS take aim at anyone in their sights. Lale pulls Gita up hard against a building. Another loud explosion.

"That's Crematorium 4—someone's blowing it up. We have to get out of here."

Prisoners run from the administration building and are gunned down.

"I have to get you back to your block. It's the only place you'll be safe."

An announcement over the loudspeakers: "All prisoners return to your blocks. You will not be fired upon if you go now."

"Go, quickly."

"I'm frightened, take me with you," she cries.

"You'll be safer in your own block tonight. They're bound to do a roll call. My darling, you can't get caught outside your block."

She hesitates.

"Go now. Stay in your block tonight, and go to work as normal tomorrow. You must not give them any reason to look for you. You must wake up tomorrow."

She takes a deep breath and turns to run.

In parting, Lale says, "I'll find you tomorrow. I love you."

⌒

THAT NIGHT, LALE BREAKS HIS RULE AND JOINS THE MEN, mostly Hungarians, in his block to find out what he can about the afternoon's events. It appears that some of the female prisoners working in an ammunition factory nearby have been smuggling tiny amounts of gunpowder back to Birkenau, pushed up into their fingernails. They have been getting it to the Sonderkommando, who have been making crude grenades out of sardine tins. They have also been stockpiling weapons, including small arms, knives, and axes.

The men in Lale's block also tell him of rumors about a general uprising, which they wanted to join but didn't believe it was meant to happen on this day. They have heard that the Russians are advancing, and the uprising was planned to coincide with their arrival, to assist them in liberating the camp. Lale admonishes himself for not having made friends with his block companions sooner. Not having this knowledge nearly got Gita killed. He questions the men extensively on what they know about the Russians and when they are likely to arrive. The replies are vague, but are enough to provoke slight optimism.

It has been months since the American plane flew overhead. The transports have kept coming. Lale has seen no lessening of the dedication of the Nazi machine to the extermination of Jews and other groups. Still, these latest arrivals have a more recent connection with the outside world. *Perhaps liberation is coming.* He is determined to tell Gita what he has learned and ask her to be vigilant in the office, to glean any information she can.

At last, a glimmer of hope.

24

AUTUMN IS BITTERLY COLD. MANY DON'T SURVIVE. LALE and Gita hold on to their glimmer of hope. Gita lets her block-mates know of the rumors about the Russians and encourages them to believe that they can outlive Auschwitz. As 1945 begins, temperatures plummet further. Gita cannot stop morale from ebbing away. Warm coats from the Canada cannot keep out the chill and fear of another year captive in the forgotten world of Auschwitz-Birkenau. The transports slow. This has a perverse effect on those prisoners who work for the SS, particularly the Sonderkommando. Having less work to do puts them in danger of execution. As for Lale, he has built up some reserves, but his supply of new currency is much diminished. And the locals, including Victor and Yuri, are no longer coming in to work. Construction has halted. Lale has heard promising news that two of the crematoria damaged in the explosions by the resistance fighters are not going to be repaired. For the first time in Lale's memory, more people are leaving Birkenau than are entering. Gita and her co-workers take turns processing those being shipped out, supposedly to other concentration camps.

Snow is thick on the ground on a late January day when Lale is told that Leon has "gone." He asks Baretski, as they walk together, if he knows where to. Baretski offers no answer, and warns Lale that he, too, might find himself on a transport out of Birkenau. But Lale can still make his way mostly unobserved, not required to report at roll call each morning and evening. He hopes this will keep him at the camp, but he doesn't have the same confidence that Gita will remain. Baretski laughs his insidious laugh. The news of Leon's probable death taps into reserves of pain Lale did not know he still had.

"You see your world reflected in a mirror, but I have another mirror," Lale says.

Baretski stops. He looks at Lale, and Lale holds his stare.

"I look into mine," says Lale, "and I see a world that will bring yours down."

Baretski smiles. "And do you think you will live to see that happen?"

"Yes, I do."

Baretski places his hand on his holstered pistol. "I could shatter your mirror right now."

"You won't do that."

"You've been out in the cold too long, Tätowierer. Go and get warm and come to your senses." Baretski walks away.

Lale watches him leave. He knows that if they were ever to meet on a dark night on equal terms, it would be he who would walk away. Lale would have no qualms about taking this man's life. He would have the last word.

ONE MORNING IN LATE JANUARY, GITA STUMBLES THROUGH the snow toward Lale, running toward his block, somewhere he's told her never to come near.

"There's something happening," she cries.

"What do you mean?"

"The SS, they're acting strange. They seem to be panicking."

"Where's Dana?" Lale asks with concern.

"I don't know."

"Find her, go to your block, and stay there until I come."

"I want to stay with you."

Lale pulls her off him, holding her at arm's length.

"Hurry, Gita, find Dana and go to your block. I'll come and find you when I can. I need to find out what's going on. There haven't been any new arrivals for weeks now. This could be the beginning of the end."

She turns and moves reluctantly away from Lale.

He reaches the administration building and cautiously enters the office, so familiar to him from years of obtaining supplies and instructions. Inside, it's chaos. SS are yelling at frightened workers, who cower at their desks as the SS pull books, cards, and paperwork from them. An SS worker hurries past Lale, her hands full of papers and entry books. He bumps into her, and she spills what she is carrying.

"I'm sorry. Here, let me help you."

They both bend down to gather up the papers.

"Are you all right?" he says as gently as possible.

"I think you may be out of a job, Tätowierer."

"Why? What's going on?"

She leans into Lale, whispering now.

"We're emptying the camp, starting tomorrow."

Lale's heart leaps. "What can you tell me? Please."

"The Russians, they're nearly here."

❧

LALE RUNS FROM THE BUILDING TO THE WOMEN'S CAMP. THE door to Block 29 is shut. No one is standing guard outside. Entering, Lale finds the women huddled together at the back. Even Cilka is here. They gather around him, frightened and full of questions.

"All I can tell you is that the SS appear to be destroying records," Lale says. "One of them told me the Russians are nearby." He withholds the news that the camp is going to be emptying out the next day because he doesn't want to cause further alarm by admitting that he doesn't know where to.

"What do you think the SS are going to do with us?" Dana asks.

"I don't know. Let's hope they will run off and let the Russians liberate the camp. I'll try to find out more. I'll come back and tell you what I learn. Don't leave the block. There are bound to be some trigger-happy guards out there."

He takes Dana by both hands. "Dana, I don't know what's going to happen, but while I have the chance I want to tell you how much I will always be grateful to you for being Gita's friend. I know you have kept her going many times when she has wanted to give up."

They embrace. Lale kisses her on the forehead and then hands her over to Gita. He turns to Cilka and Ivana and wraps them both in a bear hug.

To Cilka, he says, "You are the bravest person I have ever met.

You must not carry any guilt for what has happened here. You are an innocent—remember that."

In between sobs she replies, "I did what I had to do to survive. If I hadn't, someone else would have suffered at the hands of that pig."

"I owe my life to you, Cilka, and I will never forget that."

He turns to Gita.

"Don't say anything," she says. "Don't you dare say a word."

"Gita—"

"No. You don't get to say anything to me other than you'll see me tomorrow. That's all I want to hear from you."

Lale looks at these young women and realizes that there is nothing left to say. They were brought to this camp as girls, and now—not one of them having yet reached the age of twenty-one—they are broken, damaged young women. He knows they will never grow to be the women they were meant to be. Their futures have been derailed, and there will be no getting back on the same track. The visions they once had of themselves, as daughters, sisters, wives and mothers, workers, travelers, and lovers, will forever be tainted by what they've witnessed and endured.

He leaves them to go in search of Baretski and information about what the next day will bring. The officer is nowhere to be found. Lale trudges back to his block, where he finds the Hungarian men anxious and worried. He tells them what he knows, but it's of little comfort.

⬯

IN THE NIGHT, SS OFFICERS ENTER EVERY BLOCK IN THE women's camp and paint a bright-red slash down the back of each girl's coat. Once again, the women are marked for whatever fate awaits them. Gita, Dana, Cilka, and Ivana take comfort in all of them having been marked alike. Whatever happens tomorrow will happen to all of them—together they will live or die.

❧

SOMETIME DURING THE NIGHT LALE FINALLY FELL ASLEEP. He is woken by a great commotion. It takes a few moments for the noises to penetrate his groggy brain. Memories of the night the Romany were taken flood back. *What is this new horror?* The sounds of rifle shots jolt him fully awake. Putting on his shoes and wrapping a blanket around his shoulders, he cautiously goes outside. Thousands of women prisoners are being corralled into rows. There is obvious confusion, as if neither guards nor prisoners know quite what is expected. The SS pay Lale no attention as he walks quickly up and down the rows of women, who are bunched together from the cold and in fear of what is to come. Snow continues to fall. Running is impossible. Lale watches as a dog snaps at the legs of one woman and brings her to the ground. A friend reaches down to help her to her feet, but the SS officer holding the dog draws his pistol and shoots the fallen woman.

Lale hurries on, looking down the rows, searching, desperate. Finally he sees her. Gita and her friends are being pushed toward the main gates, clinging to each other, but he can't see Cilka among them, or anywhere in the sea of faces. He focuses back on Gita. She has her head down, and Lale can tell by the movement of her shoulders that she is sobbing. *At last she is crying, but I can't comfort her.* Dana spots him. She pulls Gita toward the outside of their row and points Lale out to her. Gita finally looks up and sees him. Their eyes meet, hers wet, pleading, his full of sorrow. Focused on Gita, Lale doesn't see the SS officer. He is unable to move out of the way of the rifle that swings at him, connecting with his face and sending him to his knees. Gita and Dana both scream and try to force their way back through the column of women. To no avail. They are swept up in the tide of moving bodies. Lale struggles to his feet, blood streaming down his face from a large gash above his right eye. Frantic now, he plunges into the moving crowd, searching each row of distraught women. As he gets near the gates, he sees her again—within arm's length. A guard steps in front of him and pushes the muzzle of his rifle into Lale's chest.

"*Gita!*" he screams.

Lale's world is spinning. He looks up at the sky, which seems only to be getting darker as the morning breaks. Above the noise of screaming guards and barking dogs, he hears her.

"Furman. My name is Gita Furman!"

Sinking to his knees in front of the unmoving guard, he shouts, "I love you."

Nothing comes back. Lale remains on his knees. The guard moves away. The cries of the women have stopped. The dogs cease barking.

The gates of Birkenau are shut.

Lale kneels in the snow, which continues to fall heavily. Blood from the wound in his forehead covers his face. He's locked in, alone. He's failed. An officer comes over to him. "You'll freeze to death. Come on, go back to your block."

He reaches a hand down and pulls Lale to his feet. An act of kindness from the enemy at the eleventh hour.

⁓

CANNON FIRE AND EXPLOSIONS WAKE LALE THE NEXT MORN-ing. He rushes outside with the Hungarians, to be greeted by panicked SS and a chaos of prisoners and captors on the move, seemingly oblivious to each other.

The main gates are wide open.

Hundreds of prisoners walk through, unchallenged. Dazed, weak from malnourishment. Some stumble around and then choose to return to their block to escape the cold. Lale walks through gates he has been through hundreds of times before on the way to Auschwitz. A train is standing nearby, belching smoke into the sky, ready to leave. Guards and dogs begin rounding up men and pushing them toward the train. Lale gets caught up in the scrum and finds himself scrambling aboard. The gates of his wagon are slammed closed. He pushes his way to the side and peers out. Hundreds of prisoners are still wandering around aimlessly. As the train pulls away, he sees SS open fire on those who remain.

He stands, staring through the slats of the wagon, through the snow falling heavily, mercilessly, as Birkenau disappears.

25

GITA AND HER FRIENDS ARE ON THE MARCH WITH THOUSANDS of other women from Birkenau and Auschwitz, trudging along a narrow track through ankle-deep snow. As carefully as they can, Gita and Dana search the rows, all too aware that any straggling is dealt with by a bullet. They ask a hundred times, "Have you seen Cilka? Have you seen Ivana?" The answer is always the same. The women try to support each other by linking arms. At seemingly random times, they are halted and told to take a rest. Despite the cold they sit in the snow, anything to give their feet some relief. Many remain there when the order to move on comes: dead or dying, unable to take another step.

Day becomes night, and still they march. Their numbers dwindle, which only makes it harder to escape the watchful eye of the SS. During the night, Dana drops to her knees. She can go on no longer. Gita stops with her and for a while they are unseen, screened by other women. Dana keeps telling Gita to go on, to leave her.

Gita protests. She would rather die here with her friend, in a field somewhere in Poland. Four young girls offer to help carry Dana. Dana will not hear of it. She tells them to take Gita and go. As an SS officer advances on them, the four girls pull Gita to her feet and drag her with them. Gita looks back at the officer, who has stopped beside Dana but moves on without drawing his pistol. No shot rings out. Clearly he thinks she is already dead. The girls continue to drag Gita. They will not let her go as she attempts to break free and get back to Dana.

Through the dark, the women stumble on, the sound of random shots barely even registering now. No longer do they turn around to see who has fallen.

As day breaks, they are brought to a halt in a field by a train track. An engine and several cattle wagons stand waiting. *They brought me here. Now they will take me away*, thinks Gita.

She has learned that the four girls she is now traveling with are Polish and not Jewish. Polish girls who were taken from their families for reasons they do not know. They come from four different towns and hadn't known each other before Birkenau.

Across the field stands a lone house. Behind it, a dense wood spreads out. SS bark out orders as the train engine is stoked with coal. The Polish girls turn to Gita. One of them says, "We're going to make a run for that house. If we get shot, then we will die here, but we're not going any farther. Do you want to come with us?"

Gita stands up.

Once the girls are running, they don't look back. The act of loading thousands of exhausted women onto the train takes all the guards' attention. The door to the house is opened before they reach it. Inside, they collapse in front of a roaring fire, adrenaline and relief surging through them. Hot drinks are placed in their hands, along with bread. The Polish girls talk frantically to the homeowners, who shake their heads in disbelief. Gita says nothing, not wanting her accent to give away the fact that she isn't Polish. It's better their saviors think she is one of them—the quiet one. The man of the house says they can't stay with them, as the Germans often search the premises. He tells them to take their coats off. He takes them out behind the house. When he returns, the red slashes are gone and the coats smell of petrol.

Outside, they hear repeated shooting, and peering through the curtains, they watch as all the surviving women are finally herded onto the train. Bodies litter the snow beside the tracks. The man gives the girls the address of a relative in a nearby village, as well as a supply of bread and a blanket. They leave the house and enter the woods, where they spend the night on the freezing ground, curled up together in a vain attempt to stay warm. The bare trees provide little in the way of protection, either from being seen or from the elements.

※

It is early evening before they arrive in the next village. The sun has gone down, and the weak streetlamps cast little light. They are forced to ask a passerby for help finding the address they have been given. The kind woman takes them to the house they seek and stays with them while they knock on the door.

"Look after them," she says when the door opens, and walks away.

A woman stands aside as the girls enter her home. Once the door is closed, they explain who sent them here.

"Do you know who that was just now?" the woman stammers.

"No," one of the girls answers.

"She's SS. A senior SS officer."

"Do you think she knows who we are?"

"She's not stupid. I've heard stories about her being one of the cruelest people in the concentration camps."

An elderly woman comes out of the kitchen.

"Mother, we have some guests. These poor things were in one of the camps. We must give them something warm to eat."

The older woman makes a fuss over the girls, taking them into the kitchen, sitting them at the table. Gita can't remember the last time she sat on a chair at a kitchen table. The older woman ladles hot soup for them from a stove and then peppers them with questions. The owners decide it is not safe for them to stay here. They are afraid the SS officer will report the girls' presence.

The older woman excuses herself and leaves the house. A short while later, she returns with a neighbor. Her house has both a roof cavity and a cellar. She is willing to let the five of them sleep in the roof. With the heat from the fireplace rising, it will be warmer up there than in the cellar. They won't be able to stay in the house during the day, though, as every house can be searched at any time by the Germans, even though they seem to be re-treating.

Gita and her four Polish friends sleep in the roof space each night and spend the days hiding in the nearby woods. Word sweeps through the small village, and the local priest has his parishioners bring food to the house's owner each day. After a few weeks the remaining Germans are flushed out by the advancing Russian soldiers, several of whom set up house in the property directly opposite where Gita and her friends sleep. One morning, the girls are late leaving for the woods and are stopped by a Russian standing guard outside the building. They show him their tattoos and try to explain where they have been and how they are here now. Sympathetic to their plight, he offers to place a guard outside the house. This means they no longer have to spend their days in the woods. Where they live is no longer a secret, and they receive a smile or a wave from the soldiers when they come and go.

One day one of the soldiers asks Gita a direct question, and when she answers he immediately recognizes that she isn't Polish. She tells him she is from Slovakia. That evening, he knocks on the door and introduces a young man dressed in a Russian uniform but who is in fact from Slovakia. The two of them talk into the night.

The girls have been pushing their luck in staying by the fire later into the evening. A degree of complacency has set in. One evening, they are caught off guard when the front door bursts open and a drunk Russian staggers in. The girls can see their "guard" lying unconscious outside. Waving a pistol, the intruder singles out one of the girls and attempts to rip her clothes off. At the same time, he drops his trousers. Gita and the others scream. Several Russian soldiers burst into the room. Seeing their comrade on top of one of the girls, one of them pulls out his pistol and shoots him in the head. He and his comrades drag the would-be rapist from the house, apologizing profusely.

Traumatized, the girls decide they must move on. One of them had a sister living in Krakow. Maybe she is still there. As a further apology for the attack the previous night, a senior Russian soldier arranges a driver and a small truck to take them to Krakow.

⁓

THEY FIND THE SISTER STILL LIVING IN HER SMALL APART-ment above a grocery store. The flat is crowded with people, friends who had fled the city and are now returning, homeless. No one has any money. To get by, they visit a market every day and each person steals one item of food. From these pickings they make a nightly meal.

One day at the market, Gita's ears prick up at the sound of her native language being spoken by a truck driver unloading produce. She learns from him that several trucks travel every week from Bratislava to Krakow, bringing fresh fruit and vegetables. He accepts her request to travel back with them. She runs and tells the people she has been living with that she is leaving. Saying goodbye to the four friends she escaped with is very difficult. They come with her to the market and wave her off as the truck carrying her and two of her countrymen leaves in the direction of a host of unknowns. She has long accepted that her parents and two young sisters are dead, but she prays that at least one of her brothers has survived. Becoming partisan fighters for the Russians might have kept them safe.

⪻

IN BRATISLAVA, JUST AS IN KRAKOW, GITA JOINS OTHER SUR-vivors of the camps in crowded shared apartments. She registers her name and address with the Red Cross, having been told that all returning prisoners are doing this in the hope they can find missing relatives and friends.

One afternoon she looks out of her apartment window to see two young Russian soldiers jumping over the back fence into the property where she lives. She is terrified, but as they come closer she recognizes her two brothers, Doddo and Latslo. Running down the stairs, she flings open the door and hugs them with all her strength. They dare not stay, they tell her. Even though the Russians liberated the town from the Germans, the locals are suspicious of anyone wearing a Russian uniform. Not wanting to spoil the brief sweetness of their reunion, Gita keeps what she knows about the rest of the family to herself. They will find out soon enough, and this is not something to be spoken of in a few snatched minutes.

Before they separate, Gita tells them how she, too, has worn a Russian uniform: it was the first clothing she was given on arrival at Auschwitz. She says she looked better in it than they do, and they all laugh.

26

L ALE'S TRAIN MOVES ACROSS THE COUNTRYSIDE. HE LEANS against the compartment wall, fiddling with the two pouches tied inside his trousers that contain the gems he's risked bringing with him. The bulk of them he left under his mattress. Whoever searches his room can have them.

Later that evening, the train grinds to a halt and rifle-toting SS order everyone to scramble out, just as they had nearly three years ago in Birkenau. Another concentration camp. One of the men in Lale's wagon jumps down with him.

"I know this place. I've been here before."

"Yeah?" Lale says.

"Mauthausen, in Austria. Not quite as terrible as Birkenau, but nearly."

"I'm Lale."

"Joseph, pleased to meet you."

Once the men have all disembarked, the SS wave them through, telling them to go and find themselves a place to sleep. Lale follows Joseph into a block. The men here are starving—skin-covered skeletons—yet they still have enough life in them to be territorial.

"Piss off, there's no room in here."

One man per bunk, each has claimed his space and looks prepared to fight to defend it. Two more blocks elicit the same response. Finally they find one with more space and claim their turf. As others come into the block, searching for a place to sleep, they call out the accepted greeting: "Piss off, we're full here."

The next morning, Lale sees men from the blocks near him lining up. He realizes he is to be strip-searched and asked for information about who he is and where he has come from. Again. From his gem pouches, he takes the three largest diamonds and puts them in his mouth. He rushes to the back of the block while the rest of the men are still gathering and scatters the remaining gems there. The inspection of the line of naked men begins. He watches the guards yanking open the mouths of those before him, so he rolls the diamonds under his tongue. He has his mouth open before the inspecting party reaches him. After a quick glance, they walk on by.

❧

FOR SEVERAL WEEKS LALE, ALONG WITH ALL THE OTHER PRISoners, sits around doing virtually nothing. Almost all he can do is watch, in particular the SS guarding them, and he tries to work out who can be approached and who must be avoided. He starts to talk occasionally to one of them. The guard is impressed that Lale speaks fluent German. He has heard about Auschwitz and Birkenau but has not been there, and wants to hear about it. Lale paints a picture removed from reality. Nothing can be gained by telling this German the true nature of the treatment of prisoners there. He tells him what he did there and how he much preferred to work than to sit around. A few days later, the guard asks him if he'd like to move to a subcamp of Mauthausen, at Saurer-Werke in Vienna. Thinking it cannot be any worse than here, and with assurances from the guard that conditions are slightly better and the commandant is too old to care, Lale accepts the offer. The guard points out that this camp does not take Jews, so he should keep quiet about his religion.

The next day the guard tells Lale, "Gather your things. You're out of here."

Lale looks around. "Gathered."

"You leave by truck in about an hour. Line up at the gate. Your name is on the list," he laughs.

"My name?"

"Yes. You need to keep your arm with its number hidden, OK?"

"I get to answer to my name?"

"Yes—don't forget. Good luck."

"Before you go, I'd like to give you something."

The guard looks perplexed.

From his mouth Lale takes a diamond, wipes it on his shirt, and hands it to him. "Now you can't say you never got anything from a Jew."

⤙

VIENNA. WHO WOULDN'T WANT TO VISIT VIENNA? IT WAS A dream destination for Lale in his playboy days. The very word sounds romantic, full of style and possibility. But he doesn't doubt that it will now fail to live up to this perception.

The guards are indifferent to Lale and the others when they

arrive. They find a block and are told where and when to get their meals. Lale's thoughts are dominated by Gita and by how he can get to her. Being shunted from camp to camp to camp—he cannot bear it much longer.

For several days, he observes his surroundings. He sees the camp commandant doddering about and wonders how he is still breathing. He chats to amenable guards and tries to understand the dynamic among the prisoners. Once he discovers that he is probably the only Slovak prisoner here, he decides to keep to himself. Poles, Russians, and a few Italians sit around all day talking with their countrymen, leaving Lale largely isolated.

One day, two young men sidle up to him. "They say you were the Tätowierer at Auschwitz."

"Who are 'they'?"

"Someone said they thought they knew you there and that you tattooed the prisoners."

Lale grabs the young man's hand and pulls up his sleeve. No number. He turns to the second man.

"What about you, were you there?"

"No, but is it true what they say?"

"I was the Tätowierer, but so what?"

"Nothing. Just asking."

The boys walk away. Lale goes back to his daydreaming. He doesn't see the approaching SS officers until they yank him to his feet and frog-march him to a nearby building. Lale finds himself standing in front of the aging commandant, who nods to one of the SS officers. The officer pulls up Lale's sleeve, revealing his number.

"You were in Auschwitz?" the commandant asks.

"Yes, sir."

"Were you the Tätowierer there?"

"Yes, sir."

"So you are a Jew?"

"No, sir, I am a Catholic."

The commandant raises a brow. "Oh? I didn't know they had Catholics in Auschwitz."

"They had all religions there, sir, along with criminals and politicals."

"Are you a criminal?"

"No, sir."

"And you're not a Jew?"

"No, sir. I'm Catholic."

"You have answered 'no' twice. I will ask you only once more. Are you a Jew?"

"No, I am not. Here—let me prove it to you." With that, Lale undoes the string holding up his trousers, and they fall to the floor. He hooks his fingers into the back of his underpants and starts to pull them down.

"Stop. I don't need to see. OK, you can go."

Pulling his trousers back up, trying to control his breathing, which threatens to give him away, Lale hurries from the office. In an outer office, he stops and slumps into a chair. The officer behind a nearby desk looks at him.

"Are you all right?"

"Yes, I'm good, just a bit dizzy. Do you know what the date is?"

"It's the twenty-second—no, wait, the twenty-third of April. Why?"

"Nothing. Thanks. Goodbye."

Outside, Lale looks at the prisoners sitting lazily around the compound and at the guards, who look even lazier. *Three years. You've taken three years of my life. You will not have one more day.* Lale walks along the back of the blocks, shaking the fence, looking for a weak point. It doesn't take him long to find one. The fence comes away at ground level, and he is able to pull it toward him. Not even bothering to see if anyone is watching, he crawls under and walks calmly away.

Forest provides him with cover from any patrolling Germans. As he walks deeper in, he hears the sound of cannons and rifle fire. He doesn't know whether to walk toward it or run the other way. During a brief cease-fire, he hears the running of a stream. To reach it he must get closer to the shooting, but he's always had a good internal compass and that direction feels right. If it is the Russians, or even the Americans, on the other side of the stream, he will gladly surrender to them. As the daylight fades into evening, he can see the flash of gunfire and cannons in the distance. Still, it is the water he wants to get to, and hopefully a bridge and a route away. When he gets there, a river confronts him rather than a stream. He looks across and listens to the cannon fire. *It must be the Russians. I'm coming your way.* Lowering himself into the water, Lale is shocked at the freezing cold. He swims slowly out into the river, careful not to disturb the water too much with his strokes in case he's seen. Pausing, he raises his head and listens. The gunfire is closer. "Shit," he mutters. He stops swimming and lets the current carry him directly under the cross fire, just another log or dead body to be ignored. When he thinks he has safely cleared the warring armies, he swims frantically to the far bank. He hauls himself out and drags his drenched body into the trees before collapsing in shivers and passing out.

27

L ALE WAKES TO THE FEELING OF THE SUN ON HIS FACE. His clothes have dried out a bit, and he can hear the sound of the river running below him. He crawls on his belly through the trees that have hidden him overnight and reaches the crest of a road. Russian soldiers are walking along it. He watches for a few moments, fearing gunfire. But the soldiers are relaxed. He decides to accelerate his plan to get home.

Lale raises his hands and steps out onto the road, startling a group of soldiers. They raise their rifles immediately.

"I am Slovak. I have been in a concentration camp for three years."

The soldiers exchange glances.

"Fuck off," one of them says, and they resume their march, one of them shoving Lale as he goes by. He stands for several minutes as many more soldiers walk past, ignoring him. Accepting their indifference, he carries on, receiving only an occasional glance. He decides to walk in the opposite direction from them, reasoning that the Russians are probably heading to engage with the Germans, so getting as far away as possible makes sense.

Eventually, a jeep pulls up alongside him and stops. An officer in the back eyeballs him. "Who the hell are you?"

"I'm Slovak. I have been a prisoner in Auschwitz for three years." He pulls up his left sleeve to reveal his tattooed number.

"Never heard of it."

Lale swallows. It is unimaginable to him that a place of such horror should not be known.

"It's in Poland. That's all I can tell you."

"You speak perfect Russian," the soldier says. "Any other languages?"

"Czech, German, French, Hungarian, and Polish."

The officer eyes him more carefully. "And where do you think you're going?"

"Home, back to Slovakia."

"No, you're not. I have just the job for you. Get in."

Lale wants to run, but he would have no chance, so he climbs into the passenger seat.

"Turn around, back to headquarters," the officer instructs the driver.

The jeep bumps over potholes and ditches, heading back the way it has come. A few miles farther on, they pass through a small village and then turn up a dirt road toward a large chalet that sits on the top of a hill overlooking a beautiful valley. They enter a large circular driveway where several expensive-looking cars are parked. Two guards stand on either side of an imposing main doorway. The jeep skids to a stop, and the driver scrambles out and opens the door for the officer in the back.

"Come with me," the officer says.

Lale scurries after him into the foyer of the chalet. He pauses, shocked by the opulence before him. A grand staircase, works of art—paintings and tapestries on every wall—and furniture of a quality he has never seen before. Lale has stepped into a world beyond his comprehension. After what he has known, it is almost painful.

The officer heads toward a room off the main foyer, indicating that Lale should follow. They enter a large, exquisitely furnished room. A mahogany desk dominates, as does the person sitting behind it. Judging by his uniform and accompanying insignia, he is a very senior Russian official. The man looks up as they enter.

"Who have we here?"

"He claims he was a prisoner of the Nazis for three years. I suspect he's a Jew, but I don't think that matters. What does matter is that he speaks both Russian and German," the officer says.

"And?"

"I thought he could be useful to us. You know, in talking to the locals."

The senior officer leans back, seems to consider this. "Put him to work, then. Find someone to guard him, and shoot him if he tries to escape." As Lale is escorted from the room, the senior officer adds, "And get him cleaned up and into some better clothes."

"Yes, sir. I think he will do well for us."

Lale follows the officer. *I don't know what they want from me, but if it means a bath and clean clothes . . .* They walk across the foyer and head upstairs to the second-floor landing; Lale notes that there are two further floors. They enter a bedroom, and the Russian goes to the closet and opens it. Women's clothing. Without a word, he leaves and enters the next bedroom. This time, men's clothes.

"Find something that fits you and looks good. There should be a bathroom through there." He points. "Clean yourself up. I'll be back in a little while."

He closes the door behind him. Lale looks around the room. There is a large four-poster bed draped in heavy covers, with mountains of pillows of all shapes and sizes; a chest of drawers he thinks might be solid ebony; a small table, complete with Tiffany lamp; and a lounge chair covered in exquisite embroidery. How he wishes Gita were here. He stifles the thought. He cannot afford to think of her. Not yet.

Lale runs his hands over the suits and shirts in the closet, both casual and formal, and all the accessories needed to resurrect the Lale of old. He selects a suit and holds it up to the mirror, admiring the look: it will be close to a perfect fit. He throws it onto the bed. A white shirt soon joins it. From a drawer he selects soft underpants, crisp socks, and a smooth brown leather belt. He finds a polished pair of shoes in another cupboard, a match for the suit. He slips his bare feet into them. Perfect.

A door leads to the bathroom. Gold fittings glisten against the white tiles that cover the walls and floor; a large stained-glass window casts pale yellow and dark-green light around the room from the late-afternoon sun. He enters the room and stands still for a long time, enjoying the anticipation. Then he runs a deep bath and lowers himself into it, luxuriating in it until the water cools. He adds more steaming water, in no hurry for his first bath in three years to end. Eventually he climbs out and dries himself with a soft towel that he finds hanging with several others on the rail. He walks back into the bedroom and dresses slowly, savoring the feel of smooth cotton, linen, and woolen socks. Nothing scratches, irritates, or hangs baggily off his shrunken frame. Clearly the owner of these clothes was slim.

He sits for a while on the bed, waiting for his minder to return. Then he decides to explore the room some more. He pulls back large drapes to reveal French windows that lead out onto a balcony.

He opens the doors with a flourish and steps outside. *Wow. Where am I?* An immaculate garden stretches out before him, lawn disappearing into a forest. He has a perfect view down onto the circular drive, and he watches as several cars pull up and deposit more Russian officials. He hears the door to his room opening and turns around to see his minder alongside another, lower-ranked soldier. He stays on the balcony. The two men join him and look out over the grounds.

"Very nice, don't you think?" Lale's minder says.

"You've done well for yourselves. Quite a find."

His minder laughs. "Yes, we have. This headquarters is a bit more comfortable than the one we had at the front."

"Are you going to tell me where I fit in?"

"This is Friedrich. He is going to be your guard. He will shoot you if you try to escape."

Lale looks at the man. His arm muscles bulge against his shirtsleeves, and his chest threatens to pop the buttons that hold it in. His thin lips neither smile nor grimace. Lale's nod of greeting isn't returned.

"He will not only guard you here but will also take you to the village each day to make our purchases. Do you understand?"

"What am I buying?"

"Well, it's not wine; we have a cellar full of that. Food, the chefs will buy. They know what they want . . ."

"So that leaves . . ."

"Entertainment."

Lale keeps his face neutral.

"You will go into the village each morning to find lovely young ladies interested in spending some time here with us in the evening. Understand?"

"I'm to be your pimp?"

"You understand perfectly."

"How am I to persuade them? Tell them you are all good-looking fellows who will treat them well?"

"We will give you things to entice them."

"What sort of things?"

"Come with me."

The three men walk back downstairs to another sumptuous room, where an officer opens a large vault set into a wall. The minder enters the vault and brings out two metal tins, which he places on the desk. In one, there is currency; in the other, jewelry. Lale can see many other similar tins shelved in the vault.

"Friedrich will bring you here each morning, and you will take both money and jewelry for the girls. We need eight to ten each night. Just show them the payment, and if need be give them a small amount of money in advance. Tell them they will be paid in full when they arrive at the chalet, and when the evening is over they will be returned to their homes safe and well."

Lale attempts to reach into the jewelry tin, which is promptly slammed shut.

"Have you struck a rate with them already?" he asks.

"I'll leave that to you to figure out. Just get the best deal you can. Understand?"

"Sure, you'd like prime beef for the price of sausage." Lale knows the right thing to say.

The officer laughs. "Go with Friedrich; he'll show you around. You can take your meals in the kitchen or your room—let the chefs know."

Friedrich takes Lale downstairs and introduces him to two of the chefs. He tells them he would prefer to eat in his room. Friedrich tells Lale that he must not go above the first floor, and even there, he is to enter no room but his own. He gets the message loud and clear.

A few hours later, Lale is brought a meal of lamb in a thick, creamy sauce. The carrots are cooked al dente and drip with butter. The plate is garnished with salt, pepper, and fresh parsley. He had wondered if he might have lost the ability to appreciate rich flavors. He hasn't. What he has lost, however, is the ability to enjoy the food before him. How can he, when Gita is not there to share it with him? When he has no idea whether she has anything to eat at all? When he has no idea . . . but he suppresses that thought. He is here now, and he must do what he has to do before he can find her. He only eats half of what's on his plate. Always save some; that is how he has lived these past years. Along with the food, Lale drinks most of a bottle of wine. It takes some effort to undress himself before he flops onto his bed and enters the sleep of the intoxicated.

He is woken the next morning by the clang of a breakfast tray being placed on the table. He can't remember if he locked his room or not. Perhaps the chef has a key. The evening's tray and bottle are taken away. All without a word.

After breakfast, he takes a quick shower. He is slipping on his shoes when Friedrich walks in. "Ready?"

Lale nods. "Let's go."

First stop, the study with the vault. Friedrich and another officer look on as Lale selects a quantity of cash, which is counted and noted in a ledger, and then a combination of small items of jewelry and a few loose gems, also noted.

"I'm taking more than I probably need because it's my first time and I have no idea what the going rate is, OK?" he says to both men.

They shrug.

"Just make sure you return anything you don't give away," the accountant officer says.

Putting the money in one pocket and the jewels in another, Lale follows Friedrich to a large garage block by the chalet. Friedrich commandeers a jeep and Lale gets in, and they drive the few miles into the village Lale came through yesterday. *Was it only yesterday? How can I feel so different already?* During the journey, Friedrich tells him they will drive a small truck in to pick up the girls in the evening. It isn't comfortable, but it's the only vehicle they have that can take twelve. As they enter the village, Lale asks, "So, where should I look for likely girls?"

"I'll drop you at the top of the street. Go into all the shops. Workers or customers—it doesn't matter as long as they are young and, preferably, pretty. Find their price, show them the payment— if they want something up-front, give them cash only. Tell them we will pick them up at six o'clock outside the bakery. Some have been before."

"How will I know if they're already attached?"

"They'll say no, I'm thinking. They might also throw something at you, so be prepared to duck." As Lale gets out, he says, "I'll be waiting and watching. Take your time. And don't do anything stupid."

Lale heads to a nearby boutique, hoping no husbands or boyfriends have gone shopping with their partners today. Everyone looks at him when he enters. He says hello in Russian, before remembering he is in Austria and switching to German.

"Hello, ladies, how are you today?"

The women look at each other. A few giggle before a shop attendant asks, "Can I help you? Are you looking for something for your wife?"

"Not exactly. I want to talk to all of you."

"Are you Russian?" a customer asks.

"No, I'm Slovak. However, I am here on behalf of the Russian army."

"Are you staying in the chalet?" asks another customer.

"Yes."

To Lale's relief, one of the shop attendants speaks up: "Are you here to see if we want to party tonight?"

"Yes, yes, I am. Have you been before?"

"I have. Don't look so frightened. We all know what you want."

Lale looks around. There are two shop assistants and four customers.

"Well?" he says cautiously.

"Show us what you've got," a customer says.

Lale empties his pockets onto the counter as the women gather around.

"How much can we have?"

Lale looks at the woman who has been to the chalet before.

"How much were you paid last time?"

She waves a diamond-and-pearl ring under his nose. "Plus ten marks."

"OK, how about I give you five marks now, another five tonight, and your choice of a piece of jewelry?"

The girl rummages through and picks out a pearl bracelet. "I'll have this one."

Lale takes it gently from her hand. "Not yet," he says. "Be at the bakery at six tonight. Deal?"

"Deal," she says.

Lale hands her five marks, which she stuffs down her bra.

The remaining girls peruse the jewelry and choose what they want. Lale gives them each five marks. There is no haggling.

"Thank you, ladies. Before I leave, can you tell me where I might find some like-minded beauties?"

"You could try the café a few doors down, or the library," one of them suggests.

"Be careful of the grandmas in the café," one woman says with a giggle.

"What do you mean, 'grandmas'?" Lale asks.

"You know, old women—some of them are over thirty!"

Lale smiles.

"Look," says the original volunteer, "you can stop any woman you meet in the street. We all know what you want, and there are plenty of us who need good food and drink even if we have to share it with those ugly Russian pigs. There are no men left here to help us. We do what we have to."

"As do I," Lale tells them. "Thank you all very much. I'll look forward to seeing you tonight."

Lale leaves the shop and leans against a wall, taking a breather. One shop, half the women required. He looks to the other side of the street. Friedrich is looking at him. He gives him a thumbs-up.

Now, where's that café? On his walk there Lale stops three young women, two of whom agree to come to the party. In the café he finds three more. He thinks they are in their low- to mid-thirties, but they are still beautiful women anyone would want to be seen with.

That evening Lale and Friedrich pick up the women, who are all waiting at the bakery as instructed. They are elegantly dressed and made-up. The agreed transaction in jewelry and cash takes place, with minimal scrutiny from Friedrich.

He watches as they enter the chalet. They are holding hands, wearing resolute expressions, and occasionally laughing.

"I'll take what's left over," Friedrich says, standing close to Lale.

Lale takes several notes and a couple of pieces of jewelry from his pockets and hands them to Friedrich, who seems satisfied that the transactions have been carried out correctly. Friedrich pockets the goods, then sets about patting Lale down, digging his hands deep into his pockets.

"Hey, careful," says Lale. "I don't know you that well!"

"You're not my type."

⁂

THE KITCHEN MUST HAVE BEEN TOLD ABOUT HIS RETURN, as his supper arrives shortly after he has entered his room. He eats and then walks out onto the balcony. Leaning on the balustrade, he watches the comings and goings of vehicles. Occasionally the sound of the partying below filters up to him, and he is pleased that he hears only laughter and conversation. Back in his room, he begins to undress for bed. Fiddling around in the cuff of his trousers, he finds the small diamond he has placed there. He takes a single sock out of the drawer and stuffs the diamond into it before retiring for the night.

He is woken a few hours later by laughter and chatter coming through his balcony doors. He steps outside and watches as the women clamber aboard the truck for the trip home. Most seem intoxicated, but none looks distressed. He goes back to bed.

⁂

FOR THE NEXT SEVERAL WEEKS, LALE AND FRIEDRICH make their twice-daily trips into the village. He becomes well-known there; even women who never come to the chalet know who he is and greet him in passing. The boutique and the café are his two favorite places, and soon women gather there at the time they know he will arrive. His regulars often greet him with a kiss on the cheek and a request for him to join the party that night. They seem genuinely upset that he never does.

One day in the café, Serena, a waitress there, says loudly, "Lale, will you marry me when the war is over?" The other girls there giggle, and the older women tut.

"She's fallen for you, Lale. She doesn't want any of those Russian pigs, no matter how much money they have," one of the customers adds.

"You are a very beautiful woman, Serena, but I'm afraid my heart belongs to someone else."

"Who? What's her name?" asks Serena indignantly.

"Her name is Gita, and I am promised to her. I love her."

"Is she waiting for you? Where is she?"

"I don't know where she is right now, but I'll find her."

"How do you even know if she's alive?"

"Oh, she's alive. Have you ever just known something?"

"I'm not sure."

"Then you've never been in love. I'll see you girls later. Six o'clock. Don't be late."

A chorus of goodbyes follows him out the door.

⁓

THAT NIGHT, AS LALE ADDS A LARGE RUBY TO HIS WAR CHEST, a terrible homesickness overtakes him. He sits on his bed for a long time. His memories of home have been tainted by his memories of the war. Everything and everyone he cared for is now only visible to him through glasses darkened by suffering and loss. When he manages to pull himself together, he empties the sock onto his bed and counts the gems he has managed to smuggle over the weeks. Then he wanders out onto the balcony. The nights are getting warmer and several of the partygoers are out on the lawn, some lounging about, others playing a kind of game of tag. A knock on his bedroom door startles him. Since the first night, Lale has locked his door whether he is in the room or not. Rushing to open the door, Lale sees the gems on his bed and quickly pulls the covers over them. He doesn't spot the latest ruby falling onto the floor.

"Why was your door locked?" Friedrich asks.

"I do not want to find myself sharing my bed with one of your colleagues, several of whom, I have observed, have no interest in the girls we bring them."

"I see. You are a good-looking man. You know they would reward you handsomely if you were so inclined."

"I'm not."

"Would you like one of the girls? They've already been paid."

"No, thanks."

Friedrich's eye is caught by a sparkling from the rug. He bends down and picks up the ruby. "And what is this?"

Lale looks at the gem, surprised.

"Can you explain why you've got this, Lale?"

"It must have gotten caught in the lining of my pocket."

"Really?"

"Do you think I would have left it there for you to find, if I had taken it?"

Friedrich considers him. "I suppose not." He pockets it. "I'll return it to the vault."

"What did you want to see me about?" Lale asks, changing the topic.

"I'm being transferred tomorrow, so you'll be doing the morning run and pickup on your own from now on."

"You mean with someone else?" asks Lale.

"No. You've proven you can be trusted; the general's very impressed with you. Just keep doing what you're doing, and when it's time for everyone to leave here, there might even be a little bonus for you."

"I'm sorry to see you go. I've enjoyed our conversations in the truck. Look after yourself; there's still a war going on out there."

They shake hands.

Once Lale is alone, securely locked in his room, he gathers up the gems on his bed and puts them back in the sock. From the closet he chooses the nicest-looking suit and puts it aside. He lays a shirt and several pairs of underpants and socks on the table, and slots a pair of shoes underneath it.

THE NEXT MORNING LALE SHOWERS AND DRESSES IN HIS CHO-sen clothes, including four pairs of underpants and three pairs of socks. He puts the sock containing the gems into his inside jacket pocket. He takes one last look around his room and then makes his way to the vault. Lale helps himself to his normal amount of money and jewels and is about to leave when the accountant officer stops him.

"Wait. Take extra today. We have two very senior officers from Moscow arriving this afternoon. Buy them the best."

Lale takes the extra money and jewels. "I might be a little bit late coming back this morning. I'm going to the library, as well, to see if I can borrow a book."

"We've got a perfectly good library here."

"Thanks, but there are always officers in there, and . . . well, I still find them intimidating. You understand?"

"Oh, OK. As you wish."

Lale walks into the garage and nods to the attendant, who is busy washing a car. "Lovely day, Lale. Keys are in the jeep. I hear you're going alone today."

"Yes, Friedrich's been transferred; sure hope it isn't to the front."

The attendant laughs. "Just be his rotten luck."

"Oh, I've got permission to be back later than usual today."

"Want a bit of action for yourself, do you?"

"Something like that. See you later."

"OK, have a good day."

Lale hops casually into the jeep and drives away from the chalet without looking back. In the village, he parks at the end of the main street, leaves the keys in the ignition, and walks away. He spots a bicycle leaning outside a shop and casually wheels it away. Then he hops on and cycles out of town.

A few miles away, he is stopped by a Russian patrol.

A young officer challenges him. "Where are you going?"

"I have been a prisoner of the Germans for three years. I am from Slovakia and I am going home."

The Russian grabs hold of the handlebars, forcing Lale to dismount. He turns away from the soldier and receives a firm kick up the butt.

"The walk will do you good. Now fuck off."

Lale walks on. *Not worth arguing.*

Evening arrives, and he does not stop walking. He can see the lights of a small town ahead and picks up his pace. The place is crawling with Russian soldiers, and even though they ignore him, he feels he must move on. On the outskirts of town he comes across a railway station and hurries over to it, thinking he might find a bench to lay his head down for a few hours. Walking out onto a platform, he finds a train but no signs of life. The train fills him with foreboding, but he represses the fear and walks up and down, peering inside. Carriages. Carriages designed for people. A light in the nearby station office catches his attention, and he walks toward it. Inside, a stationmaster rocks on a chair, his head dropping forward as he fights the need to sleep. Lale steps back from the window and fakes a coughing fit before approaching with a confidence he doesn't really feel. The stationmaster, now awake, comes to the window, opening it just enough for a conversation.

"Can I help you?"

"The train, where is it headed?"

"Bratislava."

"Can I travel on it?"

"Can you pay?"

Lale pulls the sock from his jacket, extracts two diamonds, and hands them to him. As he does so, the sleeve on his left arm rides up, revealing his tattoo. The stationmaster takes the gems. "The end carriage—no one will bother you there. It's not leaving until six in the morning, though."

Lale glances at the clock inside the station. *Eight hours away.*

"I can wait. How long is the journey?"

"About an hour and a half."

"Thank you. Thank you very much."

As Lale is heading for the end carriage he is stopped by a call from the stationmaster, who catches up to him and hands him food and a thermos.

"It's just a sandwich the wife made, but the coffee's hot and strong."

Taking the food and coffee, Lale's shoulders sag and he can't hold back the tears. He looks up to see that the stationmaster also has tears in his eyes as he turns away, heading back to his office.

"Thank you." He can barely get the words out.

⁓

DAY BREAKS AS THEY REACH THE BORDER WITH SLOVAKIA. AN official approaches Lale and asks for his papers. Lale rolls up his sleeve to show his only form of identification: 32407.

"I am Slovak," he says.

"Welcome home."

28

BRATISLAVA. LALE STEPS OFF THE TRAIN INTO THE CITY where he has lived and been happy, where his life should have been playing out for the last three years. He wanders through districts he used to know so well. Many are now barely recognizable due to bombing. There is nothing here for him. He has to find a way back to Krompachy, some two hundred and fifty miles away; it will be a long trip home. It takes him four days of walking, interspersed with occasional rides in horse-drawn carriages, a bareback ride on a horse, and a ride on a tractor-drawn cart. He pays, when he needs to, the only way he can: a diamond here, an emerald there. Finally he walks down the street he grew up on and stands across from his family home. The palings of the front fence are gone, leaving just the twisted posts. The flowers, once his mother's pride and joy, have been strangled by weeds and overgrown grass. Rough timber is nailed over a broken window.

An elderly woman comes out of the house opposite and stomps over to him.

"What do you think you're doing? Away with you!" she screams, brandishing a wooden spoon.

"I'm sorry. It's just . . . I used to live here."

The old lady peers at him, recognition dawning. "Lale? Is that you?"

"Yes. Oh, Mrs. Molnar, is that you? You . . . You look . . ."

"Old. I know. Oh my lord, Lale, is it really you?"

They embrace. In choking voices they ask each other how they are, without either letting the other answer properly. Finally, his neighbor pulls away from him.

"What are you doing standing out here? Go on in, go home."

"Is anyone living there?"

"Your sister, of course. Oh, my—she doesn't know you're alive?"

"My *sister*! Goldie is alive?"

Lale runs across the street and knocks loudly on the door. When no one answers immediately, he knocks again. From inside he hears, "I'm coming, I'm coming."

Goldie opens the door. At the sight of her brother, she faints. Mrs. Molnar follows him inside as he picks his sister up and lays her on a sofa. Mrs. Molnar brings a glass of water. Cradling Goldie's head lovingly in his arms, Lale waits for her to open her eyes. When she comes to, he offers her the water. She sobs, spilling most of it. Mrs. Molnar lets herself out quietly as Lale rocks his sister, letting his own tears flow, too. It is quite some time before he can speak and ask the questions he so desperately wants answers to.

The news is bleak. His parents were taken away only days after he left. Goldie has no idea where they went, or if they are still alive. Max went off to join the partisans and was killed fighting the Germans. Max's wife and their two small boys were taken—again, she does not know where to. The only positive news Goldie has to offer is her own. She fell in love with a Russian, and they are married. Her name is now Sokolov. Her husband is away on business and is due back in a few days.

Lale follows her into the kitchen, not wanting to let her out of his sight, as she prepares a meal for them. After they have eaten, they talk late into the night. As much as Goldie pushes Lale for information about where he has been for the past three years, he will only say he has been in a work camp in Poland and that he is now home.

The next day he pours his heart out to both his sister and Mrs. Molnar about his love for Gita and how he believes she is still alive.

"You have to find her," Goldie says. "You must look for her."

"I don't know where to start looking."

"Well, where did she come from?" Mrs. Molnar asks.

"I don't know. She wouldn't tell me."

"Help me to understand this. You have known her three years, and all that time she told you nothing about her origins?"

"She wouldn't. She was going to tell me on the day she left Birkenau, but everything happened too quickly. All I know is her last name: it's Furman."

"Well, that's something, but not much," his sister chides him.

"I've heard that people are starting to come home from the camps," says Mrs. Molnar. "They are all arriving in Bratislava. Maybe she's there."

"If I need to go back to Bratislava, I need transport."

Goldie smiles. "So what are you doing sitting here, then?"

In the town, Lale asks everyone he sees with a horse, bike, car, or truck if he can buy it from them. They all refuse.

As he is starting to despair, an old man comes toward him in a small cart drawn by a single horse. Lale steps in front of the animal, forcing the man to rein it in.

"I'd like to buy your horse and cart," he blurts out.

"How much?"

Lale pulls several gems from his pocket. "They are real. And worth a lot of money."

After inspecting the treasure, the old man says, "On one condition."

"What? Anything."

"You have to take me home first."

A short while later Lale pulls up outside his sister's house and proudly shows off his new means of transport.

"I haven't got anything for him to eat," she exclaims.

He points to the long grass. "Your front yard needs mowing."

That night, with the horse tethered in the front yard, Mrs. Molnar and Goldie set about making meals for Lale to take on his journey. He hates saying goodbye to them both so soon after arriving home, but they won't hear of him staying.

"Don't come back without Gita," are the last words Goldie says as Lale climbs into the back of the cart and is nearly thrown out by the horse taking off. He looks back at the two women standing outside his family home, each with an arm around the other, smiling, waving.

⁓

FOR THREE DAYS AND NIGHTS, LALE AND HIS NEW COMPANION travel down broken roads and through bombed-out towns. They ford streams where bridges have been destroyed. They give rides to various people along the way. Lale eats sparingly from his rations.

He feels profound grief for his scattered family. At the same time, he longs for Gita, and this gives him the sense of purpose he needs to carry on. He must find her. He has promised.

When he eventually arrives back in Bratislava, he goes immediately to the train station. "Is it true that survivors from the concentration camps have been coming home?" he asks. He is told it is, and is given the train schedule. With no idea where Gita might have ended up—not even which country—he decides the only thing to do is meet every train. He thinks about finding somewhere to stay, but a strange man with a horse is not an attractive proposition as a lodger, so he sleeps in his cart in whatever spot of vacant land he can find, for as long as it takes for the horse to eat the grass or for them to be moved along. He is often reminded of his friends in the Romany camp and the stories they told him about their way of life. It is nearing the end of summer. The rain is frequent but doesn't deter him.

For two weeks, Lale loiters at the train station as each arrival pulls in. He walks up and down the platform, approaching every disembarking woman. "Were you in Birkenau?" On the few occasions he gets a yes, he asks, "Did you know Gita Furman? She was in Block 29." No one knows her.

One day the stationmaster asks him if he has registered Gita with the Red Cross, who are taking the names of the missing and of those who have returned and are seeking loved ones. With nothing to lose, he heads into the city center to the address he has been given.

⌒

GITA IS WALKING DOWN THE MAIN STREET WITH TWO FRIENDS when she sees a funny-looking cart being drawn by a horse. A young man stands casually in the back.

She steps out onto the road.

Time stands still as the horse stops of its own volition in front of the young woman.

Lale climbs down from the cart.

Gita takes a step toward him. Still he doesn't move. She takes another step.

"Hello," she says.

Lale drops to his knees. Gita turns around to her two friends, who are looking on in astonishment.

"Is it him?" one of them calls out.

"Yes," says Gita. "It is him."

Clearly Lale is not going to move, or is incapable of moving, so Gita walks to him. Kneeling down in front of him, she says, "In case you didn't hear me when we left Birkenau, I love you."

"Will you marry me?" he says.

"Yes, I will."

Lale sweeps Gita up into his arms and kisses her. One of Gita's friends comes over and leads the horse away. Then, with Gita's arms around Lale's waist and her head resting on his shoulder, they walk away, merging into the crowded street, one young couple among many in a war-ravaged city.

EPILOGUE

L ALE CHANGED HIS NAME TO SOKOLOV, THE RUSSIAN LAST name of his married sister—a name more readily accepted than Eisenberg in Soviet-controlled Slovakia. He and Gita were married in October 1945, and they set up home in Bratislava. Lale started importing fine fabrics—linen, silk, cotton—from throughout Europe and Asia. He sold these on to manufacturers desperate to rebuild and reclothe their country. With the Soviet Union having reunified Slovakia with the Czech Republic and creating Czechoslovakia under their influence, Lale's business was, according to him, the only one not immediately nationalized by the communist rulers. He was, after all, providing the very materials the government hierarchy wanted for their personal use.

The business grew; he took on a partner, and profits increased. Once again, Lale began wearing stylish clothing. He and Gita dined at the best restaurants and vacationed at resorts around the Soviet Union. They were strong supporters of a movement to establish a Jewish state in Israel. Gita in particular worked quietly behind the scenes, obtaining money from wealthy locals and arranging for it to be smuggled out of the country.

When the marriage of Lale's business partner ended, his exwife reported Lale and Gita's activities to the authorities. On April 20, 1948, Lale was arrested and charged with "exporting jewelry and other valuables from Czechoslovakia." The arrest warrant continued: "As a result, Czechoslovakia would have suffered untold economic losses and Sokolov would have obtained for his unlawful and marauding action significant values in money or possessions." While Lale had been exporting jewelry and money, there was nothing financial in it for him. He had been giving money away.

Two days later, his business was nationalized and he was sentenced to two years in Ilava Prison, a place that had become famous for holding political prisoners and German prisoners after the war. Lale and Gita had been smart enough to stash some of their wealth. With contacts in the local government and judiciary, Gita was able to bribe officials to help. One day, Lale received a visit in prison from a Catholic priest. After a while the priest asked the prison officials to leave the room so he could hear Lale's confession, which was sacrosanct and for his ears only. Alone, he told Lale to start acting as though he were going mad. If he did a good enough job, the officials would have to get a psychiatrist to see him. Before too long, Lale found himself in front of a psychiatrist, who told him he was going to arrange for him to be given leave to go home for a few days before he "went over the edge and couldn't be brought back."

A week later, he was driven to the apartment where he and Gita lived. He was told he would be picked up in two days to complete his sentence. That night, with the help of friends, they slipped out the back of their apartment building with a suitcase each of possessions and a painting that Gita refused to leave behind. The painting is of a Romany woman. They also took a large amount of money to give to a contact in Vienna who was destined for Israel. Then they hid behind a false wall in a truck taking produce from Bratislava into Austria.

At a given time on a given day, they walked along a platform at the Vienna train station looking for a contact they had never met. Lale described it as like something out of a le Carré novel. They muttered a password to several single gentlemen until finally one gave the appropriate response. Lale slipped a small briefcase of money to him, and then he disappeared.

From Vienna they traveled to Paris, where they rented an apartment and for several months enjoyed the cafés and bars of the city returning to its prewar self. Seeing Josephine Baker, the brilliant black American singer and dancer, perform at a cabaret was a memory Lale would always carry with him. He described her as having "legs up to here," indicating his waist.

With no work available for non-French citizens, Lale and Gita decided to leave France. They wanted to go as far away from Europe as possible. So they bought fraudulent passports and set sail for Sydney, where they landed on July 29, 1949.

On the ship over, they befriended a couple who told them about their family in Melbourne, with whom they intended to live. That was enough to persuade Lale and Gita to settle in Melbourne, too. Once again, Lale entered the textile trade. He bought a small warehouse and set about sourcing fabrics locally and abroad to sell on. Gita decided she wanted to be part of the business, too, and enrolled in a dress-design course. She subsequently started designing women's clothing, which added another dimension to their business.

Their greatest desire was to have a child, but it simply would not happen for them. Eventually, they gave up hope. Then, to their great surprise and delight, Gita got pregnant. Their son, Gary, was born in 1961, when Gita was thirty-six and Lale was forty-four. Their lives were full, with a child, friends, a successful business, and holidays on the Gold Coast, all supported by a love that no hardship had been able to break.

The painting of the Romany woman Gita brought with them from Slovakia still hangs in Gary's house.

W HEN I WAS ASKED TO WRITE AN AFTERWORD FOR THE BOOK, it was a very daunting request. Memories at so many different levels kept flooding my mind, and I was unable to get started. Do I talk about food, which was a primary focus for both my parents but especially my mother, who took pride in a fridge filled with chicken schnitzels, cold cuts, and myriad cakes and fruit? I remember her devastation when at the age of eleven I went on a major diet. On Friday night she served me my traditional three schnitzels, and I'll never forget the look on her face when I placed two of them back in the tray. "What's wrong? Is my cooking no good anymore?" she asked. It was very hard for her to register that I could no longer eat the quantity I used to. To compensate for this, when my friend came over he said hello to me and went straight to the fridge. This made her very happy. Our home was always inviting and accepting of everyone. Both Mum and Dad were very supportive of any and all hobbies and activities that I wanted to try, and keen to introduce me to everything—skiing, travel, horse riding, parasailing, and more. They felt they were robbed of their own youth and did not want me to miss out on anything.

Growing up, it was a very loving family life. The devotion my parents had to each other was total and uncompromising. When many in their circle of friends started getting divorced, I went to my mother and asked her how she and my father had managed to stay together for so many years. Her response was very simple: "Nobody is perfect. Your father has always taken care of me since the first day we met in Birkenau. I know he is not perfect, but I also know he will always put me first." The house was always full of love and affection, especially for me, and after fifty years of marriage to see them both cuddling, holding hands, and kissing—I believe this has allowed me to be a very outwardly loving and caring husband and father.

Both my parents were determined that I should know what they went through. When the TV series *The World at War* started, I was thirteen, and they made me watch it by myself every week. They were unable to watch it with me. I remember when they were showing live footage of the camps I looked to see if I could spot my parents. That footage is stuck in my mind even now. My father was comfortable with talking about his adventures in the camp, but only on the Jewish festivals when he and the men would sit around the table and chat about their experiences—all of which were fascinating. Mum, however, said nothing of the details except on one occasion when she told me that in the camp when she was very sick her mother had come to her in a vision and told her, "You will get better. Move to a faraway land and have a son."

I'll try to give you some insight into how those years affected them both. When my father was forced to close his business when I was sixteen, I came home from school just as our car was being towed away and an auction sign going up outside our home. Inside, my mum was packing up all our belongings. She was singing. Wow, I thought to myself, they have just lost everything and Mum is singing? She sat me down to tell me what was going on and I asked her, "How can you just pack and sing?" With a big smile on her face she said that when you spend years not knowing if in five minutes' time you will be dead, there is not much that you can't deal with. She said, "As long as we are alive and healthy, everything will work out for the best."

Certain things stuck with them. We would be walking along the street and Mum would bend down and pluck a four- or five-leaf clover from the ground, because when she was in the camp if you found one and gave it to the German soldiers, who believed they were lucky, you received an extra portion of soup and bread. With Dad, it was the lack of emotion and heightened survival instinct that remained with him, to the point even when his sister passed away he did not shed a tear. When I asked him about this, he said that after seeing death on such a grand scale for so many years, and after losing his parents and brother, he found he was unable to weep—that is, until Mum passed away. It was the first time I had ever seen him cry. Most of all, I remember the warmth at home, always filled with love, smiles, affection, food, and my father's sharp dry wit. It was truly an amazing environment to grow up in, and I will always be grateful to my parents for showing me this way of life.

ACKNOWLEDGMENTS

FOR TWELVE YEARS LALE'S STORY EXISTED AS A SCREENPLAY. My vision always played out on a screen—big or small. It didn't matter. It now exists as a novel, and I get to thank and acknowledge the importance of all those who stepped on and off the journey with me, and those who stayed the distance.

Gary Sokolov—you have my gratitude and love always for allowing me into your father's life and supporting me 100 percent in the telling of your parents' incredible story. You never wavered in your confidence that I would get to this point.

Glenda Bawden—my boss of twenty-one years who turned a blind eye to my sneaking out to meet with Lale and others who were helping me develop the script. And my colleagues, past and present in the Social Work Department at Monash Medical Centre.

David Redman, Shana Levine, Dean Murphy, and Ralph

Moser at Instinct Entertainment to whom I was doing most of the "sneaking out." Thank you for your passion and commitment to this project over many years.

Lisa Savage and Fabian Delussu for their brilliant investigative skills in researching the "facts" to ensure history and memory waltzed perfectly in step. Thank you so much.

Thanks to Film Victoria for their financial support with the research undertaken for the original film script version of Lale's story.

Lotte Weiss—survivor—thank you for your support and sharing your memories of Lale and Gita with me.

Shaun Miller—my lawyer, you know how to do a deal. Thanks.

My Kickstarter backers: Thank you so much for being the first to get behind the telling of this story as a novel. Your support is greatly appreciated. You are:

Keith Tweeddale, Stephanie Chen, Bella Zefira, Thomas Rice, Liz Attrill, Bruce Williamson, Evan Hammond, David Codron, Natalie Wester, Angela Meyer, Suzie Squire, George Vlamakis, Ahren Morris, Ilana Hornung, Michelle Tweeddale, Lydia Regan, Daniel Vanderlinde, Azure-Dea Hammond, Snowgum Films, Kathie Fong Yoneda, Rene Barten, Jared Morris, Gloria Winstone, Simon Altman, Greg Deacon, Steve Morris, Suzie Eisfelder, Tristan Nieto, Yvonne Durbridge, Aaron K., Lizzie Huxley-Jones, Kerry Hughes, Marcy Downes, Jen Sumner, Channy Klein, and Chris Key.

My heartfelt thanks and gratitude to Sara Nelson at HarperCollins U.S. for your passion and drive in telling this story in the United States and Canada. I have found another soul mate who embraced Lale and Gita's story and delights in its telling.

To the talented HarperCollins team in the United States

responsible for the "production" of my novel: Katherine Beitner, Mary Gaule, Amy Baker, Mary Sasso, Megan Looney, Dori Carlson, Stacey Fischkelta, and Jimmy Locabelli, Thank you so much for your dedication on behalf of myself, Lale, and Gita.

This book and all that flows from it would not exist without the amazing, the wonderful, the talented Angela Meyer, the commissioning editor at Bonnier Publishing Australia. I will be forever in your debt, and like Lale. I feel you, too, are under my skin for all time. You embraced this story with a passion and desire to match my own. You have wept and laughed with me as the story unfolded. I saw in you someone who found herself walking in Lale and Gita's shoes. You felt their pain and their love, and you inspired me to write to the best of my ability. Thank you does not seem enough, but thank you I do.

To the London team at Bonnier Zaffre headed by Mark Smith, Kate Parkin, and Julian Shaw. You believed in this story from the beginning and are responsible for the amazing reach into other territories. Thank you so much.

To my brother Ian Williamson and sister-in-law Peggi Shea who gave me their house in Big Bear, California, in the middle of their winter for a month to write the first draft. Thanks to you and your fine accommodation, to paraphrase Sir Edmund Hillary, "I knocked the bugger off."

A special thank-you to my son-in-law Evan and sister-in-law Peggi for the small but not insignificant part you each played in my making the decision to adapt my screenplay into a novel. You know what you did!

Thanks to my brothers, John, Ian, Bruce, and Stuart, who have supported me unreservedly and remind me Mum and Dad would've been so proud.

My dear friends Kathie Fong-Yoneda and Pamela Wallace, whose love and support over the years to get this story told no matter what format, I appreciate beyond words.

To my friend Harry Blutstein, whose interest and writing tips over the years I hope I have taken on board and do you proud.

The Holocaust Museum in Melbourne where Lale took me on several occasions, acting as my "living" tour guide. You opened my eyes to the world Lale and Gita survived.

My sons, Ahren and Jared, who opened their hearts and minds to Lale and let him into our family life with love and reverence.

My daughter, Azure-Dea. Lale met you when you were eighteen, the same age Gita was when he met her. He told me he fell a little bit in love with you on that first day. For the next three years every time I saw him his opening line was "How are you, and how is your beautiful daughter?" Thank you for letting him flirt with you a little and the smile you put on his face.

To my children's partners—thank you, Bronwyn, Rebecca, and Evan.

Steve, my darling husband of forty-something years. I recall a time you asked me if you should be jealous of Lale as I was spending so much time with him. Yes and no. You were there for me when I would come home sullen and depressed at having taken on board the horror Lale shared with me. You opened our home to him and let him into our family with honor and respect. I know you will continue this journey by my side.

About the author

About the book

P.S.

Insights,
Interviews
& More . . .

*

Meet Heather Morris

HEATHER MORRIS IS A native of New Zealand, and now resides in Australia. For several years, while working in a large public hospital in Melbourne, she studied and wrote screenplays, one of which was optioned in the United States. In 2003, Heather was introduced to an elderly gentleman who "might just have a story worth telling." The day she met Lale Sokolov changed both their lives. Their friendship grew, and Lale embarked on a journey of self-scrutiny, entrusting the innermost details of his life during the Holocaust to her. Heather originally wrote Lale's story as a screenplay—which ranked high in international competitions—before reshaping it into her debut novel, *The Tattooist of Auschwitz*. ∿

Author's Note

I'M IN THE LIVING room of the home of an elderly man. I don't know him well yet, but I've quickly come to know his dogs, Tootsie and Bam Bam—one the size of a pony and the other smaller than my cat. Thankfully I've won them over, and right now they are asleep.

I look away for a moment. I have to tell him.

"You do know I'm not Jewish?"

An hour has passed since we met. The elderly man in the chair opposite me gives an impatient but not unfriendly snort. He looks away, folds his fingers. His legs are crossed, and the free foot raps a silent beat. His eyes look toward the window and the open space outside.

"Yes," he says finally, turning to me with a smile. "That's why I want you."

I relax a little. Maybe I am in the right place after all.

"So," he says, as though he is about to share a joke, "tell me what you know about Jews."

Seven-branch candlesticks come to mind as I scramble for something to say.

"Do you know any Jews?"

I come up with one. "I work with a woman named Bella. She's Jewish, I think."

I expect disdain but instead receive enthusiasm. "Good!" he says.

I've passed another test.

Next comes the first instruction. "You will have no preconceptions about what I tell you." He pauses, as though searching ▶

Author's Note (*continued*)

for words. "I don't want any personal baggage brought to my story."

I shift uncomfortably. "Maybe there is some."

He leans forward unsteadily. He catches the table with a hand. The table is unsteady, too, and its uneven leg smacks against the floor, causing an echo. The dogs wake up, startled.

I swallow. "My mother's maiden name was Schwartfeger. Her family was German."

He relaxes. "We all come from somewhere," he says.

"Yes, but I'm a Kiwi. My mother's family has lived in New Zealand for over a hundred years."

"Immigrants."

"Yes."

He sits back, relaxed now. "How quickly can you write?" he asks.

I'm thrown off balance. What exactly is he asking here? "Well, it depends on what I'm writing."

"I need you to work quickly. I don't have much time."

Panic. I had deliberately not brought any recording or writing materials with me to this first meeting. I'd been invited to hear and consider writing his life story. For now, I just wanted to listen. "How much time do you have?" I ask him.

"A little while only."

I'm confused. "Do you have to be somewhere soon?"

"Yes," he says, his gaze again returning

to the open window. "I need to be with Gita."

* * *

I never met Gita. It was her death and Lale's need to join her that pushed him to tell his story. He wanted it to be recorded so, in his words, "it would never happen again."

After that first meeting, I visited Lale two or three times a week. The story took three years to untangle. I had to earn his trust, and it took time before he was willing to embark on the deep self-scrutiny that parts of his story required. We had become friends—no, more than friends; our lives became entwined as he shed the burden of guilt he had carried for more than fifty years, the fear that he and Gita might be seen as Nazi collaborators. Part of Lale's burden passed to me as I sat with him at his kitchen table, this dear man with his trembling hands, his quivering voice, his eyes that still moistened sixty years after experiencing the most horrifying events in human history.

He told his story piecemeal, sometimes slowly, sometimes at bullet pace and without clear connections between the many, many episodes. But it didn't matter. It was spellbinding to sit with him and his two dogs, and listen to what to an uninterested ear might have sounded like the ramblings of an old man. Was it the delightful Eastern European accent? The charm of this old rascal? Was it the twisted story I was starting to make sense of? It was all of these and more. ▶

Author's Note (*continued*)

As the teller of Lale's story, I had to identify how memory and history sometimes waltz in step and sometimes strain to part, to present not a lesson in history, of which there are many, but a unique lesson in humanity. Lale's memories were, on the whole, remarkably clear and precise. They matched my research into people, dates, and places. Was this a comfort? Getting to know a person for whom such terrible facts had been a lived reality made them all the more horrific. There was no parting of memory and history for this beautiful old man—they waltzed perfectly in step.

The Tattooist of Auschwitz is a story of two ordinary people living in an extraordinary time, deprived not only of their freedom but also their dignity, their names, and their identities. It is Lale's account of what they needed to do to survive. Lale lived his life by the motto: "If you wake up in the morning, it is a good day." On the morning of his funeral I woke knowing it was not a good day for me, but that it would have been for him. He was now with Gita.

Additional Information

LALE WAS BORN LUDWIG Eisenberg on October 28, 1916, in Krompachy, Slovakia. He was transported to Auschwitz on April 23, 1942, and tattooed with the number 32407.

Gita was born Gisela Fuhrmannova (Furman) on March 11, 1925, in Vranov nad Topl'ou, Slovakia. She was transported to Auschwitz on April 13, 1942, and tattooed. She was retattooed by Lale in July when she moved from Auschwitz to Birken. There is some uncertainty regarding Gita's number, which Gary stated she had removed when she was in her sixties. Lale remembered it as 34902.

Lale's parents, Jozef and Serena Eisenberg, were transported to Auschwitz on March 26, 1942, while Lale was still in Prague. Research has uncovered that they were killed immediately upon arrival at Auschwitz. Lale never knew this. It was discovered after his death.

Lale was imprisoned in the Strafkompanie (penal unit) from June 16 to July 10, 1944, where he was tortured by Jakub. No one was expected to survive or be released from that unit.

Gita's neighbor Hilda Goldstein survived and made her way home to Vranov nad Topl'ou.

Cilka was charged as a Nazi conspirator and sentenced to fifteen years' hard labor, which she served in Siberia. Afterward, she returned to Bratislava. She and Gita met only once, in the mid-1970s, when Gita went to visit her two brothers.

In 1961, Stefan Baretski was tried for war crimes in Frankfurt and sentenced to life imprisonment. On June 21, 1988, he committed suicide in the Konitzky-Stift Hospital in Bad Nauheim, Germany.

Gita died on October 3, 2003.

Lale died on October 31, 2006. ∿

Norway

Sweden

Denmark

Baltic Sea

Prussia

East Prussia

Vistula R.

Elbe R.

Berlin

Poznań

Warsaw

Netherlands

Hanover

Oder R.

Lublin

Belgium

Rhine R.

Greater Germany

General Government

Paris

Frankfurt

Prague

Birkenau

Auschwitz

Nuremberg

Bohemia and Moravia

Krompachy

Strasbourg

Danube R.

Munich

Vienna

Vranov Nad Topľou

France

Mauthausen

Saurer-Werke

Bratislava

Saltzburg

Switzerland

Budapest

Hungary

Romania

Italy

Yugoslavia

Mainland Europe
1942–1945

Albania

KZ Auschwitz II Birkenau, 1944

- **B Ia** Frauenlager
- **B Ib** anfangs Männerlager, ab 1943 Frauenlager
- **B IIa** Quarantänelager
- **B IIb** Theresienstädter Familienlager
- **B IIc** Durchgangslager für Jüdinnen
- **B IId** Männerlager
- **B IIe** »Zigeunerlager«
- **B IIf** Häftlingskrankenlager (Männer)

»Zentrale Sauna« (»Entwesungs- und Desinfektionsanlage« von Januar 1944 an)

Kläranlage

Gaskammern und Krematorien II und III

Kläranlage

Lagerstraße, auf der sich Lale und Gita treffen; Rampe von Ende Mai 1944 an

»Entwesungs- und Desinfektionsanlagen«

Kartoffelbunker

Entkleidungs- baracken

Bunker 2

Platz, an dem Leichen verbrannt wurden

Gaskammern und Krematorien IV und V

Massengräber sowjetischer Kriegsgefangener

»Kanada II« (»Effektenlager«)

Platz, an dem Leichen verbrannt wurden

Entkleidungs- baracken

Bunker 1

Kommandantur

dritter Bauabschnitt im Bau (»Mexiko«)

SS-Unterkünfte

zweiter Bauabschnitt B II

Hauptwache mit Turm

erster Bauabschnitt B I

B Ia · B Ib · B IIa · B IIb · B IIc · B IId · B IIe · B IIf

Häftlingsküchen
Wohnblocks für Häftlinge
Latrinen und Waschräume

0   100   200   300 m

N · S

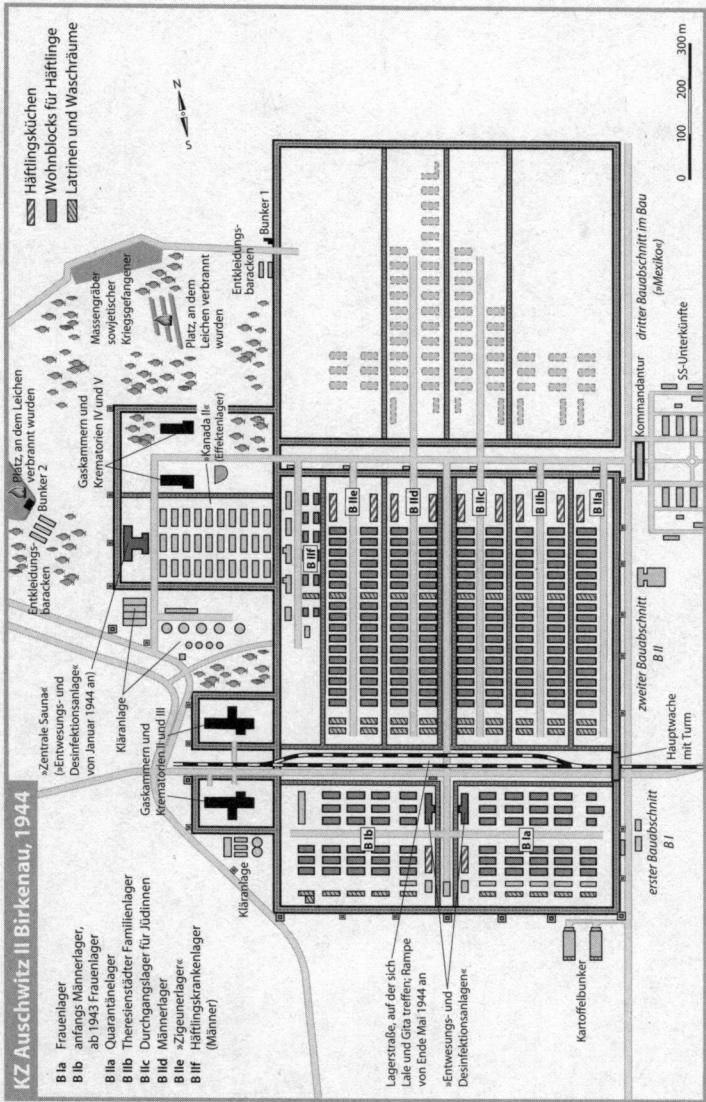